Praise fo
Shifters Unbo
By Jennifer Ashley

Pride Mates

With her usual gift for creating imaginative plots fueled by scorchingly sensual chemistry, RITA Award-winning Ashley begins a new sexy paranormal series that neatly combines high-adrenaline suspense with humor.
–*Booklist*

Primal Bonds

[A] sexually charged and imaginative tale … [A] quick pace and smart, skilled writing.
–*Publishers Weekly*

BodyGuard

Bodygaurd has passion, suspense and a touch of humor all rolled up in an enjoyable tale of romance discovered.
- Joyfully Reviewed

Wild Cat

Danger, desire, and sizzling-hot action! *Wild Cat* is a wild ride.
–Alyssa Day, *New York Times* bestselling author

Books in the
Shifters Unbound series
By Jennifer Ashley

PRIDE MATES
PRIMAL BONDS
BODYGUARD
WILD CAT
HARD MATED
"SHIFTER MADE"
(SHORT STORY PREQUEL)
MATE CLAIMED
"PERFECT MATE" (IN UNBOUND)
TIGER MAGIC

AND MORE TO COME!

Hard Mated

Shifters Unbound

Bonus Content

Shifter Made

(short story)

Jennifer Ashley

Cover design by Kendra Egert
Print cover back design by Kim Killion

Table of Contents

Chapter One

His only warning was the bone-rattling roar before several tons of enraged bear Shifter landed on him. Spike in his jaguar form rolled out of the way, twisted in a half-somersault through the dust, and came up under the bear's throat.

The crowd—under the blaze of bonfires, work lights, and lantern flashlights—roared, Shifter throats open in howls of glee.

Spike slashed upward with his fangs, catching the loose skin under the bear's chin, right above his Collar. The bear scrambled backward, swinging his head to pry loose the wildcat clinging to his throat. Spike wrapped all four huge jaguar paws around the bear's neck and hung on, biting down enough to taste blood.

Both the bear's and Spike's Collars were sparking wildly, the mechanisms designed to stop Shifters from giving in to violence.

Too late. Way too late. The beast in Spike wanted to tear into the bear's jugular and gulp down his blood, pull off his head and kick it into the middle of the ring. Spike would prove to all watchers that a wildcat could best a bear five times his size. Speed and cunning were what counted in the ring, not being as big as a two-ton pickup.

But the beast inside Spike would have to deal with it, because this was the fight club, and there were rules.

Didn't mean Spike didn't enjoy a *little* blood squeezing out of the bear. *Feel that, shithead.*

The crowd roared again, and also howled and snarled, because not everyone was in human form.

Shifters pressed forward around the ring, some still dressed, some naked and ready to shift, some already animals or half beasts. Scents both human and Shifter clogged the air, layers of excitement from the shifted females blending with the sweat of the males.

But most of all Spike smelled the bear who'd come down from Wisconsin, who thought he could best Spike, the champion of the highly illegal Shifter fight club.

Spike bit down, tasting victory, but that was before the bear grabbed Spike in his formidable front paws and jerked him from his neck.

That cost the bear, whose blood poured onto the dirt. But the grizzly lifted the squirming Spike-as-jaguar and threw him across the ring.

Spike spun in midair, corkscrewing his body. He landed on all four paws right inside the upended cinderblocks that marked the perimeter of the ring. If he'd landed outside, he'd have forfeited the match.

Cats land on their feet, dick-brain.

Spike didn't wait to decide whether the impact had hurt him. Screaming a wildcat scream, his Collar going crazy, he launched himself at the bear.

The grizzly, blood streaming down his pelt, caught Spike between his big paws, but the bear was tiring. Spike whipped his cat body around again, landing full force on the bear's back. He wrapped paws around the bear's throat and began tearing open the wound he'd already begun.

The bear bellowed in pain. He shifted to his in-between beast, half human, half bear, a monster of gigantic proportions. Spike kept ripping, blood flowed, and the bear snarled in rage.

The bear-beast collapsed, taking Spike down with him. They landed in a giant cloud of dust, Spike slamming his eyes shut before the gritty dirt blinded him.

The grizzly, back in solid bear form, made one more effort—rolling onto his back. Spike scrambled off and away before the bear could squash him flat, Spike's lithe cat's body barely taking him out of the way in time. Spike jumped to his feet, panting, ready to charge the bear again.

Two refs in human form ran between them.

"Fight's over!" one of the refs shouted. "The bear is down."

The grizzly's few supporters moaned in disappointment. The rest of the crowd screamed and hollered, humans punching the air, beasts doing victory leaps. Spike, champion of the Austin Shiftertown, had won again.

Spike stood still and caught his breath, his Collar sending fiery jolts of pain down his neck and spine.

He'd pay a long time for what he'd done in the rings tonight. Close fight. The bear was damn good.

The bear got slowly to his feet. He rose on his hind legs, higher and higher, until he flowed down into his human form—a little shorter than his bear form, but not by much. The bear—Cormac—had black hair and blue eyes and stood about seven feet tall. He spat blood from his mouth, hands on hips, catching his breath like Spike did.

Spike stretched his forepaws into the air and let himself become human, himself tall enough at six foot six. He kept his arms up, acknowledging his victory, and his fans filled the place with noise.

Cormac came across the ring, Collar sparking with residual arcs, and gave Spike a nod. "Good fight," he said, his voice rasping.

He stuck out his hand. Spike clasped it, promising himself not to grip too hard, and Cormac clapped Spike on the shoulder. The Shifter had no malice in his eyes, only approval for Spike's technique and stamina.

That was the problem with bears. They were so damn affable—when they weren't trying to kill you.

"Good fight," Spike said back. He kept his words light, his handshake strong, pretending he didn't want to fall onto the soft dirt of the ring and pass out. A few gallons of water poured down his throat wouldn't hurt either.

Cormac turned away to his friends—Ronan the Kodiak bear and his family—and a woman ran to Spike with a sports bottle.

Spike grabbed the bottle and upended a stream of water into his mouth before he realized two things.

First, the woman who'd handed him the bottle was human, and second, he'd never seen her here before.

She had black hair cut short but wildly curly, blue eyes that looked back at him in perfect equanimity, a round face that was cute rather than pretty, and lips that any male, human or Shifter would want to sink a kiss onto. Her plump body had nice curves that she didn't much hide behind a button-down shirt, sexily-cut lace tank, and jeans that rested low on her hips.

Shifter groupie? Maybe, but she didn't have the obsessed look, nor did she wear a fake Collar or paint on whiskers or anything like that.

On the other hand, Spike was standing next to her wearing nothing but his tattoos, sweat, and the blood from the fight. The woman kept her gaze on Spike's face, not even flicking it to his very naked body.

Spike upended the bottle, squirted water onto his face, and rubbed his hand over his cheeks and jaw. A shower was going to feel good.

He was also antsy, adrenaline still up in spite of the Collar's efforts. A nice roll on the sack would be great too, and here was this sweet little morsel, handing him water and looking fine in a Texas-cowgirl kind of way.

Not that Spike usually went for humans. He had to be too careful in bed with human women, because things could get wild and wicked. Shifters females were more resilient, more used to male Shifters and what they wanted.

But there was something Spike liked about this human.

"Who are you, sweetheart?" he asked.

"My name's Myka. Myka Thompson. You don't know me, but you know Jillian."

Jillian. Jillian. Who the hell was Jillian?

"You *knew* her, I should say," Myka said. "For one night at least. Five years ago. Shifter bar. You were a Shifter, she was a Shifter groupie ..." She trailed off, one hand moving before she returned it to her shapely hip.

Memory came to him. Five years ago, sure. Spike had been *very* drunk that night, but Jillian had been the hottest thing he'd seen in a long, long time. She'd been more than willing—in fact, she'd almost dragged him to that hotel room—and Spike had waived his avoidance of humans for her. "Red-headed little thing, fiery. Yeah, I remember her."

He'd never seen Jillian again. Spike liked to date his ladies for more than a night, much more than a night, but the phone number Jillian had given him had been disconnected, and she'd not come to the bar again.

Some humans were like that. They wanted a taste of the beast, but they didn't want anything long-term with a Shifter.

"How's she doing?" Spike asked. He grabbed a towel he'd left on a box outside the ring and rubbed his wet face. The towel came away filthy and bloody. He needed a shower and some bandages. Shifters healed quickly, but Spike was going to be in for a sore night.

"She's dying," Myka said.

Spike jerked back to her, towel dangling from his grasp. *"What?"*

"I said, Jillian's dying. She wants to see you, but you have to come with me now."

Chapter Two

Hospitals sucked. Myka hated them. Their pale rooms were filled with soft electronic sounds that told you that the person in the hospital bed, the person you loved, was dying. Plus, the overriding scent of antiseptic never could quite mask the mixture of bodily odors and illness.

Broke Myka's heart to see Jillian in that bed, her body that once had enticed every male in Hill Country wasted, her red hair thin and dry against the white sheets. Her blue eyes were washed out under the fluorescent lights, her skin tinged with gray.

Jillian smiled at Myka over the foot of the bed as Myka led in Spike, which couldn't be his real name. Spike, tall and Shifter, in jeans and T-shirt, his black hair buzzed into almost nonexistence, tatts of wildcats marking him up and down his arms, gazed down at Jillian in shock and grief.

Grief? Jillian was nothing to Spike, was she? He'd had to dredge her out of his memory when Myka had said her name. Jillian hadn't mentioned Spike at all until their shocker of a conversation this morning. She'd sent Myka to Shiftertown to find him, and hadn't *that* been fun?

Shifters. There was a reason they were Collared and made to live in Shiftertowns. Myka couldn't understand the women who longed to sleep with them. Too much excitement for this girl, thank you. Training horses gave her all the time she needed with animals, had taught her enough about animals that she didn't much want to be around ones that could turn human.

Shiftertown had been almost deserted, Spike not at home in the modest bungalow to which Jillian had sent her. Casual conversation with some humans in a little bar outside the perimeter of Shiftertown led Myka to the abandoned hay barn out east of town, and there she'd found the Shifters in all their wild glory at their so-called fight club.

The way Spike had beat the shit out of that bear Shifter was evidence enough of why humans wanted to contain them. They weren't even supposed to be able to fight like that—the Collars were designed to stop them. If Myka had been a good citizen, she'd report the illicit three-ringed fight club and all the Shifters there betting on their favorites.

But she hadn't been a good citizen since the day the system had given ten-year-old Myka into the custody of Randall, the stepfather from hell. Randall had been very good at charming judges, social workers, and anyone else who came along. Couldn't bear to be separated from Myka, he'd said, after Myka's mother had died, in a hospital room just like Jillian's. Randall had gotten himself appointed Myka's legal guardian, and nine long years of hell had ensued, until the day of Randall's death.

Jillian produced a thin smile as she looked over the foot of the bed at Spike. "You came. Thank you."

"Yeah."

That was the first word he'd spoke since he'd followed Myka out of the barn into the cool of the night so she could drive him here. Not *What happened? Why is she asking for me?* Just stone silence in the cab of her pickup.

Silent, sure, but his presence was weighty. This was a *Shifter*, for crying out loud, big, tough, able to break tiny young women like Jillian in half with one hand. Yet he stood there looking down at Jillian in the bed as though someone had sledgehammered him between the eyes and he hadn't remembered to fall down yet.

"I don't have a lot of time," Jillian said, her voice a faint whisper. A far cry from the girl who'd balanced on top of a rail fence at the rodeo a year ago, screaming for her favorite bull rider. She'd slept with him too. Men usually took one look at Jillian and became her devoted slaves.

"I have a gift for you," Jillian said.

She held out her hand, and Spike reached down and took it. He didn't hold her hand awkwardly—he closed it between his two big ones, as though trying to comfort her.

"What?" he asked, his voice a quiet rumble. Even a Shifter could feel the dampening presence of the hospital room.

"Myka will show you. Myka and my mom. I don't know what else to do, all right?"

Jillian pressed down on his hand, the movement so weak that Myka saw it only because a tendon moved on Jillian's wrist.

Spike nodded. What was in his eyes, Myka couldn't see, because his gaze was fixed on Jillian.

"Myka, go get my mom, okay? I asked her to wait down the hall."

Myka didn't want to leave Jillian alone with the Shifter. Jillian let her stare go steely, which she was good at, even while dying. "Myka? *Okay?*"

Spike turned his head and looked at Myka, and for the first time, Myka got the whole connection of his Shifter gaze. Spike's eyes were dark brown, his pupils black, windows into nothing.

No, not nothing. An intense something. Myka saw wildness inside him, the beast that had charged a bear four times his size and sunk his teeth into the big animal's neck. Spike's throat was singed where his Collar had shocked him, but the shocks hadn't slowed him down a millisecond. This was an animal who looked for his prey's weakness and went for it.

Myka did *not* want to leave him alone in here with Jillian.

But Jillian had hours to live, not days, the cancer taking away the last of what she had been.

Myka made herself turn around and leave, walking rapidly down the corridor to the little room where Jillian's mom Sharon waited, surrounded by vending machines, a television that blared a news channel, and other tense people who'd come to see their families.

Sharon got rapidly to her feet and followed Myka out. "Damn, I need a cigarette. Jillian kicked me out when you called from the parking lot, but I couldn't go outside with …" She wriggled her arm, jostling what she was pulling.

"I don't like this," Myka said.

"I know. But it's what Jillian wants, and I think she's right."

Myka had to shut up, because they'd entered Jillian's room again. Spike swung around, inhaling sharply.

His eyes changed to Shifter—brown tinged with gold, the pupils slits—as his gaze riveted on the small boy Sharon gripped by the hand.

At four years old, Jordan had lost his baby chubbiness and was turning into a sturdy, strong-boned lad. He had dark hair brushed with blond and brown, and dark brown eyes framed with black lashes. Until Myka had seen Spike looking at her with the same eyes, she'd doubted Jillian's claim.

Jillian drew a breath to speak, but Sharon shook her head, seeing it was too much for her. She walked Jordan forward.

"This is your son," Sharon said, her voice heavy from too many years of smoking. "So says Jillian."

"He is, Mom," Jillian's whisper came.

Jordan stared up at Spike, who filled the room not only with his presence, but with the bulk of him. Though smaller than the bear-man he'd fought, Spike was still big—six and a half feet tall, arms as big as a wrestler's and covered in tatts that disappeared inside his T-shirt, shaved head on a muscular neck encased by an inch-thick Collar. Jordan's soft mouth hung open, his small teeth white in the moisture behind his lip.

Spike stared back at Jordan just as hard, the shock mutual.

"Jordan," Jillian said from the bed. "Do your trick for Mommy."

Jordan, caught in the spell of Spike's gaze, remained frozen for another moment. Then he looked away and stripped off his shirt. Almost proudly, he shoved down his pants and underwear and stood without clothes, as unashamed as the Shifters had done at the hay barn.

The little boy lifted his arms over his head, closed his eyes, then gave a little squeak as his body changed shape.

His legs bent and became haunches, his little feet morphed into awkwardly big paws. Jordan's hands became paws before his arms did, the smooth spotted pelt sliding down to join the one that rose up his chest. His face elongated into a cat's nose, ears popped up on his head, and his eyes became rounder, fuller, eyelashes and whiskers growing swiftly. The fur that covered him was dark yellow with the broken black bands of a jaguar.

In only a few seconds, Jordan dropped to all fours and let out a tiny wildcat yowl.

The suspicion on Spike's face turned to amazement then a hungry longing. Before Myka could stop him, he bent down and scooped up the cub between his big hands.

He lifted Jordan to his eye level, staring at the cub, who wriggled and squirmed but not in alarm.

They studied each other, Shifter and cub, the big man's eyes wide, the cub's unworried. Jordan opened his mouth and emitted another little growl.

"I named him Jordan," Jillian said. "He's yours. Take care of him for me, all right?"

Spike didn't take his eyes from Jordan. Myka saw the pulse in Spike's neck, the hard beats pressing under the Collar.

Sharon waited, her fingers playing with the clasp on her cigarette case. Myka waited too, for Spike to deny it, to tell Jillian to prove it, to bail the hell out of there. Men didn't like suddenly to be told that they were fathers, didn't want to be held accountable for whatever grew from their sperm.

Spike lifted Jordan higher. Jordan's paws hung down from Spike's giant hands, his tail snaking around Spike's wrist.

"My cub," Spike said. "My cub." His voice rose to a deep roar that shook the window across the room. "My *cub.*"

"Yes," Jillian whispered, then her eyes drifted closed, and she slid back into her morphine sleep.

Chapter Three

Jillian never woke again. She slipped away around two in the morning. Spike didn't see her go, because he'd been sent to the waiting room with Jordan while Myka and Sharon stayed with Jillian. Spike was alone with Jordan now, the other people who'd been waiting having gone home or to sleep elsewhere in the hospital.

Jordan slept in Spike's lap on top of Spike's wadded-up sweat jacket, the boy back in human form and dressed again.

Holy Mother Goddess, he had a cub.

Made total sense for Spike to take the kid back to Shiftertown. Jillian's mom would never be able to hide the fact that Jordan was Shifter, and she wouldn't know how to raise a Shifter cub anyway. And if someone found out about Jordan being a

Shifter, humans would step in and take him the Goddess knew where.

No. He's *mine!*

Wherever this protectiveness had come from, Spike didn't care. Jillian had been smart to send for him. Spike could take Jordan home, watch over him, raise him, and keep him from harm. Sean Morrissey, the second-in-command of Shiftertown and its Guardian, had access to a database he called the Guardian Network, and could futz birth certificates and paperwork and make everything seem legit. Sean was talented with that stuff. If humans thought to question where Jordan had gone, they'd see him as a registered Shifter with Spike as his father. Jillian, with her interest in Shifters, had probably known that could be done.

He had a *cub.*

In spite of the tragedy—Jillian had been a sweet little thing, and far too young to pass—Spike's mouth kept wanting to spread into a smile.

That is, until Myka walked in, a scowl on her face.

"She's gone," Myka said curtly.

Spike touched his chest, which had constricted with pain, then lifted his fingers to the sky. "The Goddess go with her."

Myka eyed Spike in complete distrust. Spike rested his hand on top of the sleeping Jordan's back. Myka was *not* going to take Jordan away from him.

"So you want to keep him then?" Myka asked.

"Well, yeah, I do. I'm his dad."

She kept staring at him, arms folded, which pushed her breasts to the top of her cute tank top. "That doesn't mean you'll be a good father. You have other kids?"

"No." Again Spike caressed Jordan's back. "Just him."

"Sharon and I have been taking care of him fine between us. Jillian lived with her mom. Jordan's used to us, and Sharon's his grandmother."

She didn't get it, did she? "If humans found out he was Shifter, they'd take him away from her," Spike said. "He'll need to shift, to run, to be his wildcat. He won't be able to help himself. In Shiftertown, he'll be safe."

Myka let out a sigh. "I know that. But it's taken me a long time to talk myself into letting him go to a male Shifter. Isn't there a woman in Shiftertown he can live with? Someone you know who could take care of him—and let us see him whenever we want?"

Spike growled. "Let another family take care of my son? Screw that. Anyway, there's my grandmother. She can help me look after him."

"Your grandmother lives with you?"

"Yeah, why wouldn't she?"

Myka's lips pressed together then released into a forward push, as though she contemplated deep thoughts.

"How do you know for certain that he's your cub?" she asked. "Jillian told me you were the only Shifter she slept with, but she might have been lying for her own reasons. She sure went to Shifter bars a lot."

Spike had never seen Myka at one. "I take it you're not into Shifters."

"No."

Spike lifted Jordan, who weighed next to nothing, and cradled him against his chest as he stood up.

"Markings. His coat. He's got my family's markings."

Again the stare, the assessment. What the hell was with her?

Finally Myka let out a sigh. She dug a tiny notebook out of her big purse and scribbled something down. She tore out a piece of paper and held it out to him.

"This is my phone number. You call me if Jordan needs anything, or when the novelty of being a father wears off and you want to give him back."

Like hell he would. Spike only looked at her, making no move to take the paper. Besides, he'd have to disturb Jordan to do it.

Myka clenched her jaw, took the last step forward, and slid the paper into the top of Spike's jeans pocket. Her fingers were warm through the denim, firm, strong.

Myka snatched her hand back and turned away so fast her purse swung and smacked her in her ass. The shapely ass that swayed as she hurried to the door again. "I have to take Sharon home and help her with … everything. You need a ride back to Shiftertown?"

Spike caressed his cub's back again. "I can call for one."

"Fine." She hesitated again. "Be discreet when you leave?"

"Why the hell wouldn't I be?"

Another dithering second, Spike scenting Myka's sharp worry. Finally, she opened the heavy door and walked out. Spike heard her footsteps clicking down the hall, as though she were determined not to let herself turn back.

Spike walked out of the hospital ten minutes later, holding Jordan under the hooded jacket he now wore. He'd gone down back stairs and through empty corridors, avoiding all humans as he made for the dark parking lot. Jordan felt right nestled against his side, his little fists gripping Spike's shirt, as though he knew, even in his sleep, that Spike was his new protector.

Cell phone use hadn't been allowed on Jillian's floor, so Spike had turned his off. In the dark and chilly parking lot, he turned it on again to find five missed calls from Liam's number and the phone ringing again.

"Spike, where the *fuck* are you, lad?" The Shiftertown leader's Irish baritone came flooding over the line. "We have a situation. Get back here. Now."

"I have one too," Spike said, his voice calm. "I'm gonna need a ride home."

*** *** ***

"So what's the sitch?" Spike asked Sean Morrissey as they sped away from the hospital in Sean's father's small white pickup.

Jordan was still hidden under Spike's jacket but was an obvious lump on his right side. Even if Sean hadn't noticed the lump, he would be able to scent Jordan.

"What the hell is that?" Sean asked.

Spike couldn't keep the pride from his voice, though he had an almost crazed need to hide Jordan from all eyes until they reached home. "My cub."

Sean jerked the wheel, narrowly avoiding running into another car. "What?"

"My cub." Spike was torn between laughing at the expression on Sean's face or growling.

Shifters of old had stolen each other's females and cubs, and males had put rival males' cubs to death so they wouldn't grow up to become threats. Sean had a mate and cub of his own, and these were more civilized times, but instincts died hard. Spike didn't like the way Sean kept trying to look at Jordan. He pulled his coat closed and gave Sean a warning look.

"What has Liam so bothered?" Spike asked. "What does he expect me to do?"

Spike was a tracker. That meant he worked for the Shiftertown leader as bodyguard, watcher, and fighter, finding trouble before it could escalate into a problem. Liam, as Shiftertown leader, trusted his trackers implicitly. Had to. Liam couldn't be everywhere, and the Austin Shiftertown was large, covering three species, two dozen or so clans, and many prides and packs within those clans.

Spike's pride family was small—he and his grandmother Ella the only survivors—and they were the only jaguar-type Felines around as well. Shifter Felines had been bred from all species, but families and clans tended toward one type of cat more than others. The extensive Morrissey clan, for example, were lions. The Morrissey clan had made Spike and his grandmother honorary members when Spike and Ella had first come to Texas, because all Shifters had to be part of a clan to survive.

Which was how Spike had found himself in the position of tracker to the previous clan leader, Fergus, who at the time had also been the leader of the San Antonio Shiftertown. *Previous* meaning *now dead.* Spike had never taken a mate, never had a cub, and with the limited number of Shifter females available, Spike thought he never would.

And now here was a cub of his body, born of a single night with a human, clinging to him, depending on him.

The sudden responsibility both elated him and made him viciously protective.

Sean turned his attention to the road, but he remained tense. "The situation is that gobshite, Gavan Thibault. Your old friend."

Friend was stretching it. Spike, Nate, and Gavan had been the three top henchmen for Fergus, until Fergus's untimely demise about a year ago. Spike and Nate had moved to the Austin Shiftertown to work for Liam, while Gavan had stayed in San Antonio with the new, and much calmer, leader there.

"What was up with him?" Spike asked, his attention only marginally on the problem. Gavan was a shithead and unimportant at the moment.

"He was up at the fight club whinging on about how the fights should be to the death, because we have too many Shifters around, and we need to start weeding out the weak. Typical 'back-to-nature' Shifter shite."

True, some Shifters liked to moan about how everything had been better in the good old days, when Shifters had roamed free and lived in secret from humans. They'd also been starving, dying out, and killing each other for survival.

No decent beer or TV in the wild either. In this captivity, Shifters weren't allowed cable or HD, but they were good at finding ways around the restrictions.

"Dad and Ronan made Gavan back down, but we thought you were still there," Sean said. "But you were at the hospital. Picking up your cub? What the hell?"

Sean in addition to being Liam's younger brother, was the Shiftertown's Guardian, which meant he carried a big sword—tucked behind the seat—with which he dispatched the souls of dying Shifters. The Shifter's body dissolved to dust when the sword went through the heart, releasing the soul and ensuring that the physical remains were undefiled. The idea of being buried or cremated in the human way sent a shudder of horror through every Shifter.

Sean's status put him above Spike in the dominance chain. With pinning looks from his Irish blue eyes, Sean was trying to make Spike open up about Jordan.

But this was too new, too wondrous. Jordan was his, something private, something family. Jordan belonged to *his* pride, not the Morrisseys.

Spike would have said nothing at all until they got to Shiftertown, except that Jordan woke up. Not only did he wake up, the kid jumped inside Spike's jacket, and then he shifted.

Baby jaguar claws penetrated Spike's flesh. The claws were nowhere near the size and deadliness of a full-grown wildcat's, but it was like having ten needles driven straight into his side. Blood flowed, and Spike couldn't stop his yelp.

Jordan took the opportunity to spring out of Spike's coat and land on the dashboard, his little claws scrabbling as he tried to balance against the moving truck. His clothes had ripped and hung in shreds. Jordan crouched in confused terror, eyeing

Sean, who stared at the cub in amazement until the pickup nearly ran up the back of an SUV sitting at a traffic light.

Sean hit the brakes. Jordan lost his hold on the dash and shot through the air. Spike caught him in both hands, and found himself struggling to hold on to a squirming ball of fur.

Jordan then did what any terrified little cat might do, and the scent filled the closed air of the pickup.

"Shit!" Spike held Jordan away from him. "Shit, shit, *shit!*"

"Stop saying that, man!" Sean cried. "Or he'll do that too!"

The wet stream continued out of Jordan, half catching in Jordan's shredded jeans, half all over Spike and the seat of the pickup.

"Damn it, this is Dylan's truck," Sean shouted. He squealed around the SUV and through the streets, charging around the last corner and into Shiftertown. He slowed the truck as the road became a lane passing old bungalow houses with deep yards and porches, mostly full of Shifters enjoying the October night.

Sean cranked down his window while Spike kept a grip on Jordan, who was writhing and fighting. Spike was the champion fighter of South Texas, rarely losing a battle in the ring, and here he was, barely able to hold on to a cub ten times smaller than him, while said cub peed a river.

Jordan gave his little body a sharp wrench, twisted himself free of Spike, scrambled across the dash, and dove out Sean's open window. Sean stood on the brakes, and Spike was out of the truck before it stopped.

Jordan disappeared into the shadows between houses, but Spike was Shifter, and he could see the little wildcat running full speed into the green beyond. Spike sprinted after him, slowed down by thick motorcycle boots, not made for running.

Goddess, what a night. Jordan ran on, the scent of terror in his wake. Behind him, Sean was calling Spike's name, and Spike wished his friend would shut the fuck up a minute.

Nothing for it. Spike braced himself on the bole of a tree, shed his boots, stripped out of his clothes, and shifted to his wildcat.

As though Jordan sensed Spike's change, he sped up. The cub rocketed around trees and through yards, sprinting around houses and down tiny black alleyways. If he got out of Shiftertown, Spike's human brain said, he could be hit by a car, or shot, or at best grabbed and taken to the human police.

Spike's wildcat brain, taking over, said, *Get him.*

Plenty of Shifters witnessed the chase. The nocturnal ones were out to enjoy the night—drinking, talking, eating, screwing in the shadows—and they stopped and stared in astonishment as Jordan zoomed by, Spike hard on his ass. Some of them, damn them, tried to help.

Spike put on a burst of speed. His breed, mostly jaguar, was better at stealth and swift movement in dark places, but if jaguars had to run, they could. Spike's body bunched and lengthened as he closed the distance between himself and his unruly cub.

He reached out and brought Jordan down with a big paw on his back, gently enough not to hurt him, but firmly enough to make him stay. *Gotcha.*

Now to get him home.

There was only one way for a Shifter in beast form to carry cubs. Spike knew he'd never keep hold of Jordan in his human hands, so he closed his big jaws around the loose skin on the back of Jordan's neck and lifted the cub from his feet.

Instantly, Jordan stilled. Whatever instinct or nerve center Spike's grip triggered, Jordan tucked his head down and curled his feet and tail up under him.

Holding Jordan high enough not to drag him on the ground, Spike carried his cub down the length of Shiftertown.

The whole damn town saw him. There was Ellison Rowe, friend and Lupine Shifter; Nate, fellow tracker; Dylan, Liam and Sean's father and the scariest Shifter in Shiftertown; Dylan's mate Glory, equally as scary; Cormac, the bear Spike had bested tonight; Ronan and Ronan's human mate; and Connor, the Morrissey nephew. They all watched Spike, the big, bad champion fighter of Shiftertown, walking down the green with a cub dangling from his jaws.

Spike went on past without looking at them and climbed the back porch of his own house. His grandmother was there, and she opened the screen door for him, open-mouthed in shock. Spike walked inside with his burden and dropped the cub onto the spread of the living room rug.

Chapter Four

"Spike, what the hell?" Ella Reyes, Spike's grandmother, stood wide-eyed, her hand still on the screen door.

Jordan sprang to his feet and ran for the back door, but Ella slammed it shut. The cub hit the screen, which creaked but held, then he pushed off it and dashed back through the kitchen. The little jaguar leapt onto and across the counters, scattering everything in his way. Pans, dishes, and silverware clattered to the floor, and a coffee cup exploded into fragments and hot liquid.

Spike, still his wildcat, grabbed Jordan when he jumped down again, getting a paw on him as Jordan scrambled for his footing on the vinyl floor.

No! Spike's growl held weight. Jordan stopped squirming and looked up at Spike with fear in his eyes.

Spike eased the pressure without losing the firmness. Jordan subsided, his little body quivering.

"Spike," Ella said, arms folded as she stood in the center of the kitchen. "I ask you again: *What the hell?*"

Under Spike's paw, Jordan shifted slowly back into the form a four-year-old boy, his tattered clothes a pool of fabric on the floor.

Spike shifted to human, his big body folded in on itself, his hand still on Jordan. "This is Jordan. He's my son."

"Your *what*?"

"Son. Cub. My kid."

Ella didn't argue. No debating whether Jordan was really Spike's son. She'd seen the markings too. "Who is the mother? What clan? You didn't make a mate-claim—I'd know that."

"She was a human. A groupie—or at least she might have been. She's gone."

Ella understood what he meant, because her eyes took on a look of sorrow. "I'm sorry, Spike."

"I didn't know her. Only for the night."

Jordan looked from Spike to Ella, his shoulder engulfed by Spike's big hand. "I don't like it here," he said. "Where's my mom?"

"In the Summerland," Spike said, as gently as he could.

"Where's that? I want to go too."

Spike turned his grip into a caress. "Not yet. Someday." Not for a long, long time if Spike had anything to say about it.

"I don't want to stay here."

Jordan's brows drew together in belligerent male-Shifter fashion. The kid wasn't about to cry. He was ready to growl and storm, relieving his bewilderment by lashing out at those nearest him.

"You have to," Spike said. "I'm your dad. That's your great-grandma."

"I don't have a great-grandma." He looked up at Ella, whose dark hair and unlined face was natural in a Shifter of two-hundred years with a hundred-year-old grandson. "What's a great-grandma?"

"Your dad's grandma," Ella explained.

The scowl deepened as Jordan wrestled with this new concept.

Ella's eyes held a spark of hope, which Spike had seen in other Shifters when offspring entered the pride. Their family would carry on. They'd survive another day.

"Can you fix him something to eat?" Spike asked her.

Ella surveyed the mess of the kitchen and made an impatient noise. "Take him out of here. I'll see what I can do."

Spike rose and scooped up Jordan. He held the lad in the crook of his arm, Jordan still glaring at him. "He needs clothes," Spike said.

"I see that. I'll call around, see what I can find."

Spike walked out of the kitchen without thanking her. Ella would know he appreciated what she did, always had. They'd moved beyond human words and phrases, body language having taken over long ago.

Spike carried Jordan upstairs to his own room and planted him on the bed. "Stay there."

Jordan didn't. By the time Spike had pulled on clean sweat pants and a shirt, Jordan had opened all the drawers of the dresser and was pawing through Spike's T-shirts. "Wanna wear one."

"They're too big for you. We'll get you some your size."

"Why do you have that all over your body?" Jordan pointed to the jaguars that chased each other up Spike's arms and over his chest to evolve into the giant spread of dragon across his back.

"They're tattoos." Spike held out one arm so Jordan could examine the body art. "Ink traced into the skin."

"My mom has a tattoo," Jordan announced. "Right above her butt."

Spike remembered that, the pretty trace of ink on Jillian's body. He suddenly wondered whether Myka had any tattoos, somewhere under the low-slung jeans and lacey tank top.

His encounter with Jillian five years ago had been brief and fiery, but Spike hadn't fallen in love. Neither had Jillian fallen in love with him. Passing time had made it pretty clear that she'd meant it to be a one-night stand, nothing more. Spike doubted she'd meant to get pregnant with Jordan, but he would be ever grateful to her for calling him in tonight instead of letting him remain ignorant.

Sean was at the back door when Spike downstairs with Jordan. Ella had cleaned up the kitchen and was making sandwiches, and she answered the door. Jordan took one look at Sean and wrapped his little arms tightly around Spike's leg.

"Your clothes," Sean said to Spike as Ella took the pile of jeans, shirt, and boots. "And something for the cub to wear, from my neighbor. Her cub's about the same age."

"Thanks, Sean."

The hilt of the Sword of the Guardian stuck up behind Sean's back, a bleak silhouette in the moonlight. "You're going to have to name him," Sean said. "And I had to tell Liam."

Name him meant that Spike had to reveal his cub in a naming ceremony, which would announce to the Shifters and the world that he had a cub. A male cub, a son. The ceremony meant that the cub was taking his place in the Shifter hierarchy, where he'd be acknowledged as belonging not only to Spike and his pride, but to his clan and Shiftertown as a whole.

The rituals were supposed to ensure the cub's acceptance into the community, but Spike sometimes wished the rituals and ceremonies would go to hell. They were supposed to strengthen the Shifters, but Spike long ago had decided that Shifters were just bad at minding their own business.

Sean left them alone, wise man, when he could have insisted on dragging Spike and Jordan over to see Liam right away. Spike would have to thank Sean with a beer later.

Jordan wouldn't put on the clothes. Ella got him into the small pair of drawstring jeans by telling him he couldn't eat unless he put something on. Alarmed, Jordan grabbed the jeans and hoisted them over his bare bottom.

Ella turned the sandwiches out on a plate, each sandwich piled high with beef, turkey, chicken, tuna, or a combination. Spike didn't know what cubs ate—did they need milk? Or was that only when they were first born? Jordan announced he was hungry and proceeded to down four sandwiches before he sat back on the kitchen floor and burped.

He'd fall asleep now, Spike thought. Worn out from the night, his mother's death, being brought to Shiftertown, and now with his belly full of food, he'd curl up and sleep it off.

No such luck. Spike and Ella ended up chasing him all over the house, from cellar to attic and back again. Jordan threw off the pants and shifted back and forth from wildcat to boy depending on what he wanted to get into or *where* he wanted to get into. And he was damned fast.

When he ended up way in the back of the pantry, a wildcat cub now, wedged between shelves and refusing to come out, Ella got out a broom and tried to pry him out. Jordan leapt away, dodging her, and scampered around the kitchen, loving the game, Ella chasing him with her newfound tool.

"Grandma!" Spike shouted. "Don't you dare hit my kid with a broom!"

"It never did *you* any harm," Ella yelled back.

Jordan laughed, evaded them, and ran on.

Spike finally tackled him in the living room. Father and son were both wildcats now, and Spike pinned the squirming boy under his body. Ella had given up and gone upstairs, the night aging.

Jordan started to quiet, soothed by Spike's warm body, his adrenaline finally running down. Spike's eyes drifted closed, the slowing staccato of Jordan's heartbeat somehow comforting.

He woke up to sun pouring in the windows. Spike had shifted to human sometime in the night, and so had Jordan. Spike had slid the pants back on the sleeping little boy, and now Spike found his arms wrapped protectively around his son.

With his eyes closed, his mouth slack, one fist on the carpet, Jordan was innocence itself. And helpless.

Spike started to move his body and stifled a groan. He ached all over. The fight coupled with the shock of finding out he had a cub made his muscles stiff and his head pound. He needed water, to hydrate, or else he needed a beer. A lot of beer.

But he couldn't get drunk while he had to take care of this little guy. Drowning himself in hops was for when his cub was safe and didn't need Spike standing guard. Which would be never. Cubs had to be protected at all times.

All times. Damn it, how could he? How did *any* Shifter do it?

They had mates, that's how. They had help. Liam had his mate Kim—a human woman, sure, but she'd proved capable. The two of them watched over their new cub with unceasing vigilance. And yet, Liam still had time to run Shiftertown, Kim to conduct her business of being a lawyer to Shifters. How the hell did they do that?

How had Spike's grandma done it? Ella had raised him alone—and in the wild—after his parents and grandfather had been slaughtered by Shifter hunters down in Mexico. Spike had been a cub, ten years old. Ella had been so huddled in grief, she'd wanted to die herself, but she'd said over and over, *If I die, who's going to take care of you?* and she'd soldiered on.

His grandmother's expression last night as she'd quit and gone to bed told him that she expected him to soldier on too.

He brushed back a strand of Jordan's hair. *Cub of my pride. Now that I've met you, how can I let you go?*

Spike very gently pressed a kiss to the top of the little boy's head.

Jordan's eyes popped open. He stared up at Spike in sleepy confusion, then his eyes cleared.

"I'm hungry," Jordan said. "Can I have breakfast?"

Goddess, what was he supposed to feed a cub for breakfast? Based on the number of sandwiches Jordan had consumed last night—a lot.

Jordan wriggled out of Spike's grasp and spread his arms. "I'm dressed. I get to eat."

Spike pressed his hand to his forehead. His temples were throbbing, not helped when the land line phone rang. Loudly.

Chapter Five

Myka spent a sleepless night, grief at watching Jillian's last breath and worry about Jordan keeping her restless.

Jillian had been adamant about giving Jordan to Spike—*who the hell named their kid* Spike? Jillian had feared what would happen if humans got wind that she was raising a Shifter child, and Myka understood her fear. A system that was so fucked up it would make a little girl live with her abusive stepfather wasn't going to be kind to a Shifter child.

Even though Myka had never been a big Shifter fan, she was aware that they were treated like second-class citizens, and she thought that unfair. There was no guarantee that Sharon would be allowed to keep Jordan if someone discovered that he was half Shifter, or that Jordan wouldn't be shipped off to some Shiftertown far away. Jillian had assured her that Shifters would have a way of keeping it quiet.

But handing him over to that inked Shifter wasn't what Myka had wanted either.

She tossed and turned, imagining all kinds of dire scenarios—Spike locking the kid into a closet, maybe beating on him to relieve his feelings, or trying to figure out how to get rid of him as soon as he could. Sure, Spike had looked intensely proud when he'd realized that Jordan was his son, but that might wear off as soon as Jordan became his usual wild self. Jillian hadn't known what to do with a kid with that much energy either.

Myka spent the night with Sharon, not wanting to leave her alone, but while Sharon slept the sleep of the emotionally exhausted, Myka lay awake or got up and paced.

In the morning, Sharon's two sisters arrived with their husbands and kids. Myka, though she more or less had been living with Sharon and Jillian these last few months, decided to leave them alone. This was a time for family.

She stopped at her small house to shower and change, then she went to the stables.

Myka knew her friends and Sharon would think her crazy for wanting to work today, but at the stables she could seek peace in turmoil. Working with the horses—Myka trained Quarter Horses to be cutters, ropers, and barrel racers for their owners—usually erased all troubles from her mind.

She'd been coming to these stables since age eleven, when a friend's mother had brought her here after school. The friend's riding instructor had let

Myka get up on a horse and take a lesson too. Myka had never looked back.

Myka nodded tightly to the two other trainers who'd come for early sessions but didn't stop to talk. She took out Carlos, the cutting horse she was currently shaping into a champion for his owner.

She warmed up Carlos with nothing more strenuous than a pleasant jog around the ring before she started the real work. Cutting horses had to respond to the slightest shift in weight or touch of the reins, in order to cut a calf from the herd or to chase it back in.

Myka started the lessons of response and reward, but she realized after only a few minutes that neither her heart nor mind was in the training. She could only think of Jordan sleeping on Spike's lap, Spike's fierce eyes, and his large hand on Jordan's back.

Damn it.

She'd made a promise to Jillian to let Spike take Jordan and not interfere. Jillian had believed with all her heart that living with Spike was best for Jordan. Myka should let it alone—decision made, deed done, none of her business.

But she couldn't wash her hands of Jordan like that.

Myka gave Carlos another jog around the ring, patting him and telling him what a good boy he was, then took him back to the barn. If she tried to train while her mind was elsewhere, she risked ruining the horse. His owner would be less than pleased, and other owners might decide to look for a more reliable trainer.

Might be a moot point anyway, because the owner of the entire stables and training center wanted to sell the place to developers. Good-bye job, good-bye stables that had given Myka the girl a haven, and Myka the adult a way to make a living.

Life sucked all over.

Myka put Carlos away, fussing over him, then she went to her pickup, scraped the dust and manure from her cowboy boots, got in and started the truck, and drove to Shiftertown.

*** *** ***

Spike hauled himself off the floor and slid on his sweat pants to answer the phone, while Jordan announced once more, at the top of his lungs, that he wanted breakfast.

The call was from Liam. "Spike, lad, I need you to help me with Gavan. Go down to San Antonio and talk to him. Casual like. Find out what he's up to, if he's going to be a threat, or just likes bellyaching. He never was happy about what happened to Fergus, and I don't need that haunting me. I know about your cub situation—which we'll talk about when you get back."

Spike's hand tightened on the phone. He was a tracker—he'd pledged all kinds of loyalty to the Shiftertown leader in return for acceptance. Didn't matter who the leader was or what he asked Spike to do, Spike did it. Without question.

But this was different. Liam was asking Spike to leave Jordan alone for hours, with only his grandmother to protect him, and go to San Antonio and meet with a guy he'd never really trusted. No way could Spike take Jordan with him to the meeting—Gavan had always had a cruel streak, and Spike wasn't letting him anywhere near his cub.

"Liam," he began.

"I wouldn't ask you, but something's going on, you know Gavan better than anyone, and I need to nip this in the bud. The lad will be all right in Shiftertown, I promise. He's safe here. I'll have Kim or Andrea drop by and look in on him later."

"I can't." The words surprised Spike even as they came out of his mouth. No one said *no* to Liam Morrissey.

"Spike. Lad."

Liam was an alpha. Even over the phone, the dominance came across that made Shifters, especially Felines, want to go down on one knee and promise him fealty. He was lead Feline, lead Shifter. The mightiest of the mighty.

"I can't," Spike repeated.

Liam's voice took on a patient tone, though the dominance thing didn't go away. "I know better than anyone that we need to look after the cubs. You talking to Gavan could help us all, lad, and every cub in Shiftertown. If Gavan's up to something, it threatens your new one as much as anyone else."

Spike closed his eyes and fought the instinctive need to obey, to say yes.

Let Dylan or Sean sort out Gavan. Why the hell did Liam need Spike to do it, *today?*

Just then Jordan ran through the kitchen, screaming, a toilet brush in his hand. Ella came charging after him with the broom again.

"I'll call you back," Spike said to Liam, and hung up the phone on Liam's startled exclamation.

Spike limped back to the living room, lifted the jeans Sean had delivered to him last night, and plucked Myka's phone number out of the pocket. As soon as he turned to reach for the phone, a pickup pulled up and stopped in front of the house. Myka herself hopped out, the October sunshine making her dark hair glow like black fire.

*** *** ***

Myka studied the house as she went up the walk. Shiftertown was nowhere near as slum-like as she'd assumed, and neither was Spike's house. He lived in a two-story bungalow, its second floor about half the size of the first, an upstairs gable poking up to make the house cozy.

A wide, old-fashioned porch wrapped around the front, chairs and a porch swing adding comfort. This was not a house for display, like the fine suburban homes Myka passed on her way across town. This house was meant to be lived in.

Myka had about ten seconds to observe all this before the front screen door slammed open and a whirlwind that was Jordan flew at her.

"Aunt Myka!"

Jordan flung his arms around her legs. Myka leaned down to him, worried, but Jordan sported a big grin as he raised his arms to her, begging to be picked up.

Myka lifted him. Jordan gave her a sticky kiss and started babbling excitedly about the house, his new great-grandmother, his new clothes, and asking when he could go home.

The door opened again and Spike walked out. In the light of day, he looked even more huge than he had last night. Spike was taller than most men Myka knew, though not lanky or bony. He was big, hard with muscle, though it was lean muscle, honed by natural strength, not protein powders.

He wore only loose workout pants that rode low on his hips and tied with a drawstring, so most of that muscle was on display. The lack of clothing showed off his tatts, a dragon's tail wrapping around his abdomen to disappear down somewhere under the drawstring. *Holy effing moley.*

Spike came off the porch, looming large as he approached. He walked right up to Myka, stopping maybe an inch from her, never mind about personal space.

Was it getting hard to breathe? No, Myka stood in the cool, fresh air, October in Austin dry and fine.

Jordan squirmed in her arms and pointed at Spike. "That's my dad." He said it proudly, no fear. "Did you know I had a dad?"

"He stays with me," Spike said. His tone was flat, no argument welcome.

"How's he doing?" Myka asked.

Instead of answering, Spike looked her over, running his gaze from her unmanageable hair to the pointed toes of her cowboy boots. Myka had put on a form-hugging tank top under a button-down shirt when she'd left the house, then thrown off the shirt when she drove over here, the day plenty warm under the sunshine.

Spike didn't pretend not to look—he ran his dark gaze from her neckline to where the fabric clung to her waist. Myka held Jordan a little closer, a shield from Spike's unnerving scrutiny.

"He's fine," Spike said, answering her question. His hard gaze broke a moment, as though he wanted to say something more, then he shut up.

Jordan squirmed to get down. Myka let him with some reluctance. Jordan ran back to the porch, jumped up on the swing, and started swinging as hard as he could. The chains creaked, but the porch swing held. The look on Spike's face as he turned to watch his son was such a mixture of worry, protectiveness, and terror that it stopped Myka in her tracks.

"I came to tell you that Jillian's funeral is Saturday," she said into the silence between them. "Sharon—Jillian's mom—thought you might like to come."

Spike glanced at her. "Best I don't."

True. A Shifter showing up at a funeral with all Jillian's family might cause some problems.

"Jordan shouldn't go either," Spike said. "He wouldn't understand."

Here Myka had to disagree. "He should be able say good-bye to his mother."

"We'll say good-bye. But in the Shifter way. Human funerals are depressing. You bury your people in the ground. Or shove them into a fire. That's just weird."

"Not much alternative, is there?"

"Jordan will give her to the Goddess, with me."

Myka hadn't been religious since she'd moved in with her stepfather at age ten, but she knew that Shifters followed some form of paganism no one really understood, though many documentaries had been made. Some of the churches around town had tried time and again to convert them, but had never made a dent.

"Come to the ritual," Spike said.

"What?" Myka blinked out of her thoughts.

"Come to the ritual with us. Say good-bye to her our way."

"I'll think about it."

Spike turned fully back to Myka, resting his hands on his hips, right above his waistband. "I have to go. I don't want to, but I don't have a choice, and I can't take him with me. Not to this."

"Have to go where?" Here it came.

"Shifter business. My job." He hesitated, giving Myka the once-over again. "My grandma can't watch him by herself. She's not use to kids, and ..."

Myka waited, wondering where the *and* led, but Spike shut his mouth again.

"Are you asking me to watch him?" Myka asked.

"Can you?"

Now he was pleading. The bad-ass warrior, who'd defeated a giant bear, for crap's sake, was asking her, near-fear in his eyes, to watch over a four-year-old so he could do ... whatever he had to do.

"What is this Shifter business?" she asked.

Spike's brows drew down. "You're nosy."

"Jordan's the son of my best friend, and she died last night. So, yeah, I'm all kinds of nosy. I used to ride horses tougher than you, so don't think I'm afraid of you."

He just stared at her, like a lion might stare at a roach who'd made the same declaration. "Does that mean you'll stay?"

"You didn't answer my question about what kind of work you do."

"Errands. I'm an errand boy."

"Yeah?" Myka looked him up and down, from all those bulging muscles to his buzzed hair and his wicked-dark eyes. "What kind of errands?"

"Anything I'm told to do. And that's all you get. Stay?"

Myka had planned to already, but she made a show of conceding. "Yes."

"Yay!" Jordan yelled from the porch. "My new great-grandma made me pancakes. Want some pancakes, Aunt Myka?"

"Pancakes? Give him a sugar high, why don't you?"

Spike looked at her as though she'd lost her mind. "Pancakes are good for him. He needs energy. He's a *Shifter*."

Myka raised her hands. Now was not the time to debate. "Just go do your thing. I'll watch him."

Spike gave her a nod, half of thanks, half of exasperation. He turned around without another word and loped back up to the porch. Gracefully. He moved with amazing precision.

He opened the screen door. Jordan hopped down from the swing and dashed inside before Spike could grab him, the kid shouting for Spike's grandmother.

Spike glanced back at Myka, still holding open the door. "Well? Aren't you coming in?"

Myka hurried up to the porch. Just before she reached the door, Spike moved ahead of her and walked into the house, the screen gently swinging shut in Myka's face. What the hell?

Spike turned around impatiently and yanked the screen door open again. "I said, aren't you coming in?"

"I was, but you cut me off."

Spike scowled down at her. He was close enough that she could smell the warmth of him, the male musk, the faint sweet of syrup from his pancakes.

"You think I'm stupid enough to let a female enter someplace ahead of me? Without me checking it out first?"

"It's your own house."

Spike kept staring at her, then he shook his head. "Goddess, I'm going to have to help Jordan unlearn all kinds of stupid shit."

Chapter Six

Spike rode down to San Antonio with Ellison, a wolf Shifter who'd decided to embrace Texas all the way, though he'd been transplanted here from Colorado twenty or so years ago. Ellison wore jeans, a big belt buckle, roach-killer cowboy boots, and a big cowboy hat. He wasn't born with his Texas drawl, but he'd sure adopted it.

Ellison drove, fast and furious as usual in his old black truck, and pried the story of Jordan out of Spike. Shifters could never mind their own damn business.

Spike had mixed feelings about leaving Jordan back there alone with Myka. Good idea? Bad? She'd seemed happy to stay, had started helping his grandmother with the breakfast dishes, and Jordan had been excited to have Myka there.

That little tank top had been sexy as hell on her. Had a little bow right at her cleavage. Perfect for Spike to tug with his teeth.

He bet she'd smell good right there too. Her scent was like warm roses, spicy and strong but not overpowering. Dipping his tongue behind the bow to taste her skin—there was a good idea. His zipper started to stretch.

"I said, that little cub's a wild one," Ellison's voice cut through the fantasy. He chuckled. "Fun to watch you running after him."

Fun. Sure. Someone without cubs couldn't understand.

Or, at least, Spike didn't think Ellison had ever had cubs. The man never talked about his life before this Shiftertown. But Spike had to worry about all kinds of shit now, from what to feed the kid to the fact that he'd have to put a Collar on him sooner or later.

Spike barely controlled his growls. The Collars were painful going on, and to subject his son to that... Damn it, he couldn't do it. He couldn't let Liam do it.

Ellison drove to a bar in the north part of San Antonio, near the National Cemetery, where Gavan, Nate, and Spike had hung out on their rare off hours back when they'd been Fergus's thugs.

It was a Shifter bar—that is, a bar that allowed Shifters to drink there. This wasn't the friendly corner bar near the Austin Shiftertown where Liam worked as a manager and Shifters came to take a load off. This was a rougher place where the human bikers eyed Shifters and were always spoiling for a fight. An uneasy truce existed, each side knowing the other could start one hell of a brawl.

Everyone in the place turned around and stared at Ellison and Spike when they walked in. They recognized Spike, but he'd ceased to become a regular, and Ellison was clearly out of place.

Spike sensed their assessments, and he assessed back. He noted the exits, how many males were between him and each door out, how many of those males were Shifters, how many human. He noted who sat where, where in the bar humans and Shifters mixed, where humans and Shifters preferred to keep to their own.

Balls clacked on a pool table in the back room. Spike and Ellison ordered beers at the long bar and drifted toward the sounds of the pool game.

Gavan, a big Feline with sand-colored hair pulled into a ponytail, stood at the head of one table, watching two other Shifters play. Spike got that the other Shifters were Lupine right away from their stink. Felines were more fastidious. Spike put up with Ellison's Lupine smell only because he was used to him, and Ellison often offered to pay for beer.

Gavan hadn't changed much since Spike had last seen him. Same lank ponytail, same granite-like face, same attitude. Gavan's family was mostly mountain lion, and his washed-out eyes held the look of a solitary hunter.

Ellison started setting up a game at the empty table farthest from Gavan, signaling he wouldn't intrude on Gavan's territory. Territory fights could extend even to corners of bar back rooms.

"What are you doing here, Spike?" Gavan asked. "Morrissey send you?"

Ellison bent to break the cluster of balls, and Spike shrugged. Scents changed with lies, and Gavan would smell a false denial.

"Doesn't matter," Gavan said, then he chuckled. "I'm entitled to my own opinions. How you been, Spike?"

Spike shrugged again, burying deep any thoughts of his new cub, but he knew Gavan would scent Jordan on him too. "Can't complain."

"I saw you fight last night," Gavan said. "You're good. You wanted to kill that bear."

"Could be."

"Not *could be*. You did. I saw it in your eyes. You backed off because you had to. The kill would have felt good, yeah?"

"Yep." No question. Of course Spike had wanted the kill. He was Shifter.

But Spike wasn't as stupid as people assumed. Most Shifters and humans looked at Spike and thought, *boneheaded fighter.* Spike let them. Easier to keep them off guard while he figured out exactly what they were up to and what to do about it.

He'd have been stupid as hell to try to go for the kill with Cormac last night. The bear had been holding back his true strength, and Spike had known it.

Bears were stronger than all Shifters—they'd learned to temper their strength in order to live in Shiftertowns with other Shifters. They had to, or they'd crush every hand they shook.

Even in the ring, in a fight to show off skill, Cormac hadn't wanted to accidentally kill Spike. Spike had won through strategy and opportunity, not strength.

If Spike had gone for the kill, today his grandmother would be lighting candles and planning a ceremony to send *him* to the Goddess. Spike wouldn't have met Myka, who wouldn't have taken him to Jordan.

Thank the Goddess the bear had held back.

Gavan looked at the two Lupines. "Beat it," he said. "I want to catch up on old times with my friend."

The Lupines looked annoyed, but Gavan out-dominated them, so they laid down their cues and strode off to the bar for more beer, pretending it was their idea.

"Let's set 'em up, Spike. And talk."

Ellison didn't consider himself part of Gavan's command. He bent over the far table and took a shot, landing two solid balls in two different holes. He set up another shot as though happy to play a solo game. Gavan said nothing, which meant he didn't care whether Ellison heard what he had to say. Interesting.

Spike shoved balls into the plastic triangle, lining it up to the top of the table, while Gavan put away the Lupine's cues. Spike lifted a cue from the rack, hefted it a few times, put it back, chose another.

"Your break," Gavan said.

Spike leaned down, set his cue, and punched the cue ball hard. Balls spun wildly across the table, a striped one falling into the far corner pocket.

Gavan watched while Spike sank three more balls. Polite of the Feline to not talk while Spike concentrated on his shots.

Spike enjoyed playing pool more than he enjoyed fighting. Fighting released tension in him, a coiled snake that had to be appeased as often as possible. Sex could ease that tension a little, but fighting, even with the Collar-shock hangover, let out his pent-up aggression so he could get on with life.

Pool, on the other hand, let him think, plan, test his skill. There was something about figuring out how to make a tricky bank shot at misaligned balls, something about the spark of triumph when hearing the correct ball thunk into the correct pocket.

This game didn't depend on strength; it depended on planning and finesse, which the jaguar wildcat inside Spike found satisfying.

He'd love to play pool with Myka, came the unexpected thought. She had the look of challenge that said she'd be interesting to play against. And if she didn't know the game well, Spike could always teach her.

He'd lean over her to show her how to hold the cue, his lips brushing her ear while he explained what to do …

The memory of her scent filled his brain, as did the feeling of her fingers in his pocket when she'd pushed in the scrap of paper with her number on it.

Spike mis-stroked, catching the cue ball wrong, and the cue ball zipped right past the ball he was trying to hit.

"Distraction," Gavan said, grunting a laugh. "Is a bitch."

Spike straightened, upending his cue in silence. Gavan took his shot, sending a solid red ball caroming off two banks and into a pocket.

"Distraction is killing us all," Gavan said as he lined up his next shot. "It's taking away our instincts, depleting us." He let fly his next shot, the balls banging together with a sound like a gunshot, a solid ball fleeing to the safety of a pocket.

Too much strength. Pool was a game of subtlety.

"I thought we were having more cubs in Shiftertowns," Spike said. He thought about Jordan, and his heart soared.

"Oh, yeah, I'm not denying that, health-wise, Shifters are doing a lot better. In the wild, I lost a mate when she brought in my cub, who died too, and I never want to live through that again. But wearing the Collars, giving in to human rules—it's not what Shifters do. Humans can't kill our instincts, no matter how much they try. But they don't need to. We're killing those instincts ourselves."

Spike nodded as though he thought hard about what Gavan said. "What are we supposed to do then? Make our dominance battles to the death? We wouldn't last long if we did."

"That's bullshit, and you know it. Dominance battles are only to the death if they need to be. Mostly the other Shifter backs down, knowing he's defeated and conceding dominance. But that's hard for *you*, isn't it?" Gavan upended his cue and stepped closer to Spike. "You're a dominant, reduced to working for another dominant. That can't sit well with you."

"I'm a tracker. It's different."

"I know. We pledge ourselves to the leader of the clan, to be their eyes and ears, their best fighters. We do it even if the leader is an asshole."

Spike wondered if Gavan referred to Fergus, for whom they'd both worked, or the new leader of San Antonio, for whom Gavan now worked.

"But this isn't the wild," Gavan said. "Liam Morrissey isn't even in your clan. Neither was Fergus."

But Liam and Fergus's clan had adopted Spike and his grandmother when they'd been brought in from the wild. Gavan knew that—he was just trying to stir Spike's anger. "Being tracker to the Shiftertown leader is a high position," Spike said, pretending not to understand what Gavan was getting at.

"Sure it is, but you're the dominant tracker, and you know it." He glanced at Ellison, another of Liam's trackers, who went on shooting pool, ignoring them. "Nate's got nothing on you, and neither does Ronan, no matter how big he is. Liam's using you, Spike. It's not disloyal to say that—it's blinking obvious. You're a fighter, my old friend. A killer at heart. I say, use it."

"To do what?"

Gavan gave him a patient look. "Let me show you something. I'm going to bet a hundred dollars that you can't make this shot." He grabbed the cue ball and positioned it at the top left corner of the table. "The orange stripe into the center left pocket."

The orange-striped ball rested near the far right pocket. Spike eyed it skeptically but nodded. "I'll take that bet."

Spike lined up his cue, aiming the cue ball at another ball that would smack itself into orange stripe, to give orange stripe enough spin to glide the other way up the table.

He shot. The second ball popped into orange stripe just right, but without enough spin. Orange stripe rolled most of the way but bumped the table just shy of the center pocket.

Spike stood up without chagrin and fished into his pocket for a wad of twenties. "Doesn't always work."

"Hang on to your cash. Let's try it again."

Gavan repositioned the balls in the same places. Spike bent over his cue again.

Gavan's body heat covered his side, the Feline's voice harsh in his ear. "How about if, this time, I tell you that if you don't make that shot, I kill your cub?"

Chapter Seven

Rage burned Spike's blood all the way to his brain. His eyes flicked to Shifter, and he shot, coming up again with his hand around Gavan's throat.

Balls slammed together, and orange stripe zipped across the table to thud into the center pocket.

Gavan grinned, even while Spike's fingers bit down. "You see?" His voice rasped. "The instinct is there. Kill. Protect. Dominate."

Ellison had straightened up, his Lupine growls filling the room. A spark leapt from Spike's Collar to his neck, a tiny bite of pain.

Spike fixed on Gavan. "This is bullshit."

"It is," Gavan said. "But look at you. Ready to kill me."

Spike made himself open his hand. He snarled as Gavan backed away and rubbed his neck.

"Tell you what," Gavan said, his breath still labored. He lowered his voice, glancing at Ellison. "You come and talk to me again, but leave your sidekick at home. You have a lot of potential, and you don't deserve to be wasted on Morrissey."

"I'm not wasting myself on your fucked-up shit either."

"I'm not telling you to. This is you for yourself. Your family. You have it, Spike. Use it. Don't let those instincts go." Gavan started to clasp Spike's shoulder, looked at his face, and lowered his hand. "Come see me. Soon."

Spike said not a word. He banged the cue to the table and left the room.

He was breathing hard, his Collar still sparking. He walked out of the bar, not waiting for Ellison, back to the bright sunshine, harsh to his Shifter eyes.

*** *** ***

"What did he say to you?" Ellison asked as he drove back through traffic rushing from San Antonio to Austin. "I heard him going on about instinct and dominance, but not what he said to make you grab him like that."

Spike ran his fingers around his warm Collar and kept his gaze out the window.

Gavan had known exactly what button to push. A threat to Spike's cub, even an abstract one, had sent him into his fighting craze. He'd been ready to kill Gavan for even thinking about threatening Jordan.

"Spike?"

"He didn't say anything," Spike said, his jaw so tight he was surprised he could speak. "Same old Shifters-are-weak-living-in-Shiftertowns bullshit."

Gavan had meant more than that, and Spike knew it, but he didn't want to talk about it.

"We need to tell Liam."

"Yeah, I know."

Gavan had been offering Spike something personal. Gavan was right—Spike was a top fighter, had the instinct to kill, and was the strongest tracker Liam had except for Ronan, the Kodiak bear. Spike never talked much, because everyone expected him to fight, not think.

But back in the old days, when Shifters had been bred for fighting for the Fae, Spike would have been top of the fighting class. The best warriors had been kept to fight the most dangerous enemies, to capture the biggest prizes, to perform the most difficult tasks.

Did it bother Spike that in the wild he'd be an elite warrior, and now he was keeping an eye on troublemakers, reporting to Liam, and relieving his frustration fighting every week in the fight club?

He had no idea. This was life. You just did it. Shiftertown wasn't ideal, but it wouldn't be forever. And anyway, no way would Spike have ever let himself work for the fucking Fae.

But now Spike had a cub. He was rushing home to that cub, or would be if traffic on the 35 wasn't such a bitch.

Ellison would want to report to Liam right away. Spike wanted to go home. He'd been away from Jordan for going on four hours, and wanted to know what the cub had been up to. And Myka would be there. The scent of her lingered on his memory, and the fantasy of teaching her pool was getting sweeter by the second.

They reached the Austin Shiftertown. No gates separated Shiftertown from the rest of the city—they passed an empty lot, and they were in.

Ellison turned his truck to the Morrisseys' street, but Spike said, "Drop me off at home first."

Ellison looked surprised. "You don't want to report?"

"You report. I have things to do."

Ellison gave Spike a long look, but took a quick turn up the block to Spike's street. "All right," he said in his Texas drawl. At least he wasn't arguing.

Ellison hadn't brought the truck all the way to a halt before Spike was out the door. His house looked quiet, but he already heard the yelling from the backyard. He waved Ellison off, and Ellison drove on, shaking his head.

Spike jogged around the house, not bothering to go inside. The noise came from the back, which meant Jordan was out there.

So were most of his neighbors. Myka stood at the base of a tree, her hands on her hips. Spike's grandmother was halfway up that tree, in her wildcat form, growling at something above her.

Three guesses as to what. The other Shifters stood by, laughing or shouting advice. Nothing dangerous then, but Spike's hackles didn't settle.

"What's going on?"

Myka turned at his harsh question. Her eyes were blue like summer skies, her lips pink and moist. Kissing those lips, in the human way, would give him a taste of sweetness, soft pressure.

The lips quirked in exasperation. "Your son's up a tree."

Spike craned his head and looked up to see that, yep, Jordan was clinging to the highest branches of the big live oak.

Spike cupped his hands around his mouth and called up. "Come down out of there, son."

Jordan didn't bother with an answer. He swayed with the treetops, his little wildcat growls proclaiming he was having a great time.

The Shifters minding Spike's business gave him all kinds of advice. *Try a saucer of milk. Call the fire department. Let him stay up there. Build him a tree house.*

Glad they were finding this so hilarious. Jordan could fall and kill himself—cubs were agile, but still awkward when young. Jordan might get scared and shift back to human on the way down, and the kid was only four years old, for the Goddess's sake.

"What you let him get up a tree for?" Spike growled at Myka.

Myka's eyes widened. "*Let* him? You have a lot to learn about kids."

He was getting that. "Grandma, come down out of there."

Ella huffed, reversed herself in the careful way of cats, and scampered to the bottom of the tree. She remained in wildcat form, sitting on her haunches and growling.

Her body language and the rumbling told Spike she was vastly irritated, and hadn't been this irritated since Spike had been a cub. *Like father, like son.*

Spike stripped off his shirt, pulled off his boots, and stripped out of his pants. One of his neighbors sent out a wolf whistle. Lupines were assholes.

Naked, Spike sauntered past Myka, who looked everywhere but at him, her eyes shining as they avoided his gaze.

Spike gave Myka another look, shifted until he was in a state between human and wildcat, and scrambled up the tree.

*** *** ***

Myka stepped back in shock as the nightmare monster moved past her and started climbing.

Spike's body remained human-ish in form, but with muscles that would have split open his clothes if he hadn't shed them. The tattoos were gone, his skin now the pelt of a wildcat, jaguar patterns all over his body. His face had the flatness of a human, the fangs of a wildcat, and the jaguar's golden eyes.

If she'd seen that beast in a dark alley, Myka would have screamed herself crazy and run like hell. Even knowing it was Spike didn't stop her heart's double-time pounding or her jolt of terror when he turned those yellow-gold eyes on her.

Spike scrambled up the tree with a grace that belied his size. He moved like a dancer—one who could pull your arms off and beat you with them.

He quickly reached Jordan, but the cub danced out of reach, playing, moving to the highest branches.

There was no way someone as big as Spike could follow him without breaking the thinning limbs and plummeting both himself and the cub to the ground. Spike flowed onto the next large branch, flattening himself on it and reaching for Jordan.

Jordan leapt again, his little wildcat body twisting away from Spike's outstretched hand. The branch on which the cub landed broke in a sudden flutter of leaves, and Jordan and the branch fell.

The cub screamed. Myka screamed. The Shifters stopped laughing and scrambled to try to catch him.

Spike reached out one long arm, snagged Jordan out of the air, and pulled him in against his chest.

Myka let out a long breath, air scraping her throat. Ella had gone completely still, her gaze fixed upward.

Spike wrapped his arm around Jordan and started descending, one branch at a time.

Myka had her hands steepled over her mouth, watching tensely as Spike came down little by little, Jordan peering over his arm. The downward journey took maybe a minute, but to Myka's clenched body, it was a lifetime.

Spike jumped down the last ten feet, landing on thickly muscled legs, his long tail whipping around to balance him. Jordan shifted back to little boy in Spike's arms and squirmed to get down.

"Aunt Myka, did you see me? I was way up there! I fell, but Dad caught me."

"Yes, I saw you." Myka lifted Jordan as Spike set him on his feet. She gave him a brief, tight hug. "Don't you ever do that again. You scared me."

Jordan gave her a puzzled look. "I was all right. Dad caught me."

"But he might not be there to catch you next time. You could have hurt yourself. No more tree climbing for you."

Jordan stared at her in surprise, then he gave her his wide-eyed, ingenuous look, lower lip starting to tremble. "I love you, Aunt Myka." He threw his arms around her and buried his face in her neck.

Myka knew damn well that he was using his adorability to get himself out of trouble. He did it all the time. Jillian used to laugh about it.

Thinking of Jillian made Myka hug the boy tighter. She looked up, her eyes moist, to see Spike standing in front of her, human once more.

Naked and human, every tatt in view. The dragon's tail went all the way to the base of his very substantial …

"Is he okay?" Spike demanded.

Jordan was perfectly fine, not even afraid. "Yes," Myka said. "This time."

"You were supposed to be watching him."

The growl in Spike's voice made Myka's temper rise. Never mind he was standing there in nothing but his ink, the man too delectable for his own good.

"I *was* watching him. But it takes an army to watch Jordan. I know that from experience."

Spike put his hands on his hips. His eyes were still Shifter—tinged with yellow, his pupils slits. "My grandma can't handle a cub all by herself. She's not young anymore."

A big wildcat paw came out and swatted Spike across his leg, followed by a snarl. One of the other Shifters laughed. "Better watch it, Spike."

Spike looked his neighbors over, his eyes going Shifter all the way. "Get the hell out of here."

The Shifters went, not in terror, but with the stroll of people who knew the amusing entertainment was over.

"We should go inside," Myka said.

Ella had already headed that way, still a jaguar, but every step, every twitch of her tail betraying her irritation.

Spike reached for Jordan. Jordan was still clinging to Myka, his breathing slowing, likely drifting off to sleep, worn out from the adventure. Myka gave Spike a glare and carried Jordan past him and to the house.

Spike got ahead of her again, leading the way through the back door. By the time Myka walked into the kitchen, Ella had disappeared upstairs to her room. Myka carried the sleeping Jordan down the hall to the small bedroom she and Ella had fixed up for him while Spike had been gone.

Spike followed her, his body heat on her back. Myka laid Jordan on the bed and gently put on the nightshirt Ella had left for him—one that had tear-away shoulders in case the boy shifted in his sleep. Jordan's eyelids fluttered once before he turned onto his stomach, pulling his limbs under him and releasing a satisfied sigh.

Myka arranged a light blanket over him and straightened up to find Spike two inches away.

He was looking at Jordan, not her, and the hollow pain in his eyes made her stop.

"Spike?" she whispered.

"Eron," he said.

"What?"

"My real name. It's Eron."

Spike reached down and stroked Jordan's hair, the movement gentle. Myka never would have thought that those blunt, fighter's hands could touch so tenderly, but the caress was everything that was tender.

Spike stood up abruptly and walked out of the room. Myka adjusted the blanket again and tiptoed after him, reaching the living room in time to see

Spike pull on his jeans and shirt, not bothering with underwear. All commando, he sat on the couch and tugged Myka down beside him.

"What am I gonna do?" he asked.

Sympathy touched Myka—the man really had no idea what he'd gotten himself into. "He's your kid, Spike—Eron. It's up to you."

"Shit."

Spike studied his hands, big and sinewy, the hands that had caught Jordan in midair without effort, then stroked his cub's hair with such lightness.

"I used to follow the rodeo circuit," Myka said. "I've seen the same look that's on your face now on guys who came off bulls that were too tough to ride. You know, the whacked-up-the-side-of-the-head look."

Spike turned his hands over and examined the scarred backs. "I never got why humans have to prove they can ride on the back of a pissed-off bull. A Shifter would just make the bull do what he wanted."

"You're changing the subject," Myka said.

"I've never had a cub before."

"No kidding."

They both went silent. Spike had pulled her to sit close to him. Their thighs touched, his large and warm.

Myka heard Ella moving around upstairs, dressing or washing up or something. She'd come down any second and break this up—wouldn't she?—before Myka couldn't handle it anymore.

"Stay here and help me take care of him," Spike said.

Myka blinked at him. "Sorry?"

"Jordan knows you, and he likes you. You helped Jillian take care of him, right?"

"Sure, but ..."

Spike looked away again, a strong, strong man who had no clue what to do. Kids did that to a person.

"Spike ... Eron ... If you really can't take care of Jordan, Jillian's mom is fine with doing it. We'll fix it up to make Jillian's mom his guardian. You can come around and teach him about being Shifter and still be his dad, but you won't have the day-to-day responsibility of taking care of him."

Myka thought Spike would let out a sigh of relief and turn a grateful gaze to her, but his body tensed, and the look on his face was one of pure rage.

"No." He got to his feet, anger in every movement. "He's my *cub*. He stays here."

"You just said you needed help."

"Help, yeah. Not for you to come and take him away from me."

Myka jumped up, her temper stirring again. "I'm not trying to take him away ... No, all right, maybe I am. You're a fighter, and a Shifter, and he was happy living with his grandma. Giving him to you was Jillian's idea, not mine. I didn't want you to have him."

"Why the hell not?"

"Because who are you? You're the guy who did a one-night stand with my best friend and got her pregnant. How does that qualify you for being a good dad?"

"I'm his *dad*. Doesn't matter if I'm a good one or not!"

"Like hell. Take it from me. I had the shittiest dad in the world. He wasn't even my dad—he was my stepfather, but he wouldn't let me go, and he made my life a living hell."

Myka snapped her mouth shut, bile boiling up inside her throat. Damn it, why had she said that?

Spike stared down her, his eyes flicking back to human, the irises warm and brown. "What did he do to you?"

"It's not important. I don't want to talk about it."

Myka felt herself closing down, shutting that part of herself away. *Don't show it, don't remember, don't feel. He's gone, you're free. It was a long time ago.*

Spike put his fingers under her chin, turning her face to him. "Tell me."

"I said, I don't want to."

He took a step closer. Now his heat floated over her—bare skin and jeans.

"He hurt you." Spike's voice gentled, the gruffness entirely gone. His dark eyes fixed on her, the compassion there startling. "I see it in you." His touch gentled too, turning to a caress.

"Yes." Myka swallowed, eyes burning. "I always tried to be the perfect kid, to do everything right, you know? I tried so hard. But I never could be good enough."

"And he beat you for it, and made you think it was your fault."

"Yeah. How did you know?"

"Because my granddad did that to me. Granddad was our clan leader, and he was half-crazy, but no one could take him down. I tried to learn to be strong so he'd like me, but he never did. He just beat on me. Took me a long time to realize that him beating on me wasn't my fault. That whatever I did, I couldn't have ever pleased him, because he was the kind of person who refused to be pleased."

After her stepfather's death, Myka had considered going to therapy, but she'd shied away from it, not wanting to bare her soul. Now Spike, a Shifter she'd just met, was baring her soul for her. "That's exactly right."

"My dad didn't hurt me," Spike said. "But he wasn't strong enough to stand up to *his* dad, and stop him. I'll never be like either of them with my son."

Myka's fingers trembled. "Promise?"

"I swear by the Goddess and the Father God and on the sacred Sword of the Guardian."

The way he said it told her that these were oaths he took seriously. Myka reached for the hand that caressed her cheek and folded her fingers around it. "Good."

He leaned closer. "I'll never hurt him, Myka."

"Good," she said again.

His breath touched her skin, his fight-worn hand closing around hers. His lips were a whisper away. Myka found herself rising on tiptoes, and she kissed him.

They stood fused, frozen for a stunned moment.

Then Spike slid a strong hand behind Myka's neck, pulled her up to him, and turned the kiss bruising.

Chapter Eight

It hurt Myka, and it didn't. Spike's kiss, his touch, opened her, shattering the barrier she'd thrust up between them—the one she thrust up between herself and everyone. Myka couldn't afford to be vulnerable ever again.

Spike's mouth was hot, his lips strong. The pressure made her open her mouth to his, welcoming the firm strokes of his tongue. He tasted her, and she tasted him back, her hands moving to his shoulders, gripping. His muscles were hard under her fingertips—pressing didn't make a dent.

The kiss was like sudden sunshine after a winter storm. The ice shards inside her couldn't withstand it. Spike held Myka hard, as though he feared she'd pull away, while his mouth pinned her and didn't let go.

Spike slid his hand down her back, kneading warmth there. Cradling her, holding on. He pulled her tighter as the wild kiss went on, her body the length of his, the hard planes of his chest pressing every inch of her breasts.

Myka's thoughts shut down, tactile senses taking over. There was only warmth, the plying of his mouth, his hands holding her, his body against hers.

For Spike's part, everything feral in him roared to the surface. Myka's scent, the feel of her body, her taste, the soft sound she made in her throat—awakened the beast. He wanted her, he needed her soft flesh against his in the night.

Her mouth was small and lush, lips forming to his. She dug at his shoulders with hard fingers, wanting to pull him into her, and Spike was happy to go. He slid his hand to her buttocks, scooping her up, need tearing at him like a crazed thing.

He tasted the pain in her and wanted to make it all better. He'd sweep her up and shut out the world, sink into the goodness of her. The curve of her buttocks under his hand beckoned his tongue, her hair warmed his fingers, and she smelled like honey and sugar. If he licked her all over, would she taste as sweet?

The floor creaked upstairs again. Myka jumped in his arms, hands sliding from his shoulders to his chest, trying to push him away.

Spike jerked her closer, hand firming on her ass. Who cared if his grandmother came down and caught them? She was Shifter; she'd understand. She knew what loneliness was.

Lonely. So lonely. Stay with me.

Myka gasped, and Spike broke the kiss.

She was breathing hard, her pupils spreading but her body shaking. His instincts screamed at him to take Myka upstairs, lock her into his room with him, and not let her go until they'd made a couple more cubs to go with Jordan. Nature wanted him to do this, and Spike's mind wasn't fighting nature too much. But there was more at stake right now.

Spike had the hardest time asking for anything, let alone pleading for it. Warrior Shifters didn't plead. They killed, they gloated over their enemy's body, they sated themselves on the first woman they saw after that, then they got up the next morning and did it all over again.

Spike caressed Myka's hand between both of his and met her eyes over it. "I need you to help me." He dredged up the word inside him. *"Please."*

Myka hesitated. She'd say no, she'd walk out, get into her pickup and drive away, leaving him watching after her, bereft. Warrior Shifters were never bereft ... which was a big, fat lie.

Myka let out her breath. It whooshed over his fingertips, sending a tingle through his veins that went straight to his cock.

"All right," she said. "I'll stay. Jordan needs looking after. For a little while."

Spike kissed her mouth again, tongue gliding over her parted lips.

A little while was fine. Gave him plenty of time.

*** *** ***

Ella came hurrying down the stairs as Myka held on to Spike's hand and wondered what she'd gotten herself into.

"Liam's coming," Ella said. "I saw him from the window. Spike, what did you do?"

"Who's Liam?"

Ella's brow furrowed, her eyes flicking to Shifter. Spike tensed again, the ease Myka had felt in him when she'd promised to stay a while vanishing. He strode to the door and opened it.

"Who's Liam?" Myka repeated.

"The Shiftertown leader," Ella said. "He'd never come here, to our territory, uninvited, if there wasn't a problem."

Myka went to Spike's side at the open door. He moved to put himself in front of her, guarding her, she realized. She peered around his large body, expecting a monster to come running up the steps, snarling and ready to kill.

What she saw was a tall man in jeans and T-shirt strolling up the sidewalk, his long body as graceful in movement as Spike's. Sunshine gleamed on his black hair, the sunglasses he wore against the bright afternoon, and the black and silver Collar around his neck.

He stopped at the base of porch steps, took off the sunglasses, and looked up at Spike with very blue eyes.

"Spike, lad, can I talk to you?"

The man asked, but his body language told Myka he expected Spike to agree. Spike's body language said that he wanted to do anything but. Her work with horses had taught her that animals didn't need words to speak volumes, and Myka saw forcefully that these two men were more animal than human.

Spike made a conceding gesture, and Liam came up the steps, in no hurry. He stopped in the middle of the porch, then his gaze moved around Spike to Myka and stayed there.

The man looking out of the blue eyes had seen many things and suffered hardships, the scars of them evident in the weight of his stare.

"Who's this?" he asked, an Irish lilt to his voice.

"Her name's Myka," Spike said. "She's under my protection."

Liam's gaze shot to Spike again, leaving Myka alone. "Oh, aye?"

"Oh, yeah."

Liam looked back at Myka and drew a sharp breath through his nostrils, then he frowned. "Not mate-claimed."

"Not yet," Spike said.

"Hmm."

Spike stepped out onto the porch. He folded his arms and stood in front of Liam, effectively blocking Liam's way into the house, not that Liam made any indication he wanted to enter. But Spike was positioned so that if Liam tried to go for Myka or Ella, he'd have to first get past Spike.

"And your cub?" Liam asked. "He's all right?"

"He's sleeping."

"Good for the lad. A little peace and quiet for you too, eh?" Liam smiled, a warm, charming smile that told Myka he could really turn it on when he wanted to. "We can do his naming this Sunday. Sound fine to you?"

"What do you want, Liam?" Spike asked.

Liam's smile dimmed, but only a little. "I always wondered what would happen if you became a dad, had a family. Now I know. You're standing there wantin' to tell me to go to hell." He chuckled. "My most loyal of trackers has found his teeth."

Spike didn't relax. He and Liam were about the same size, Spike's bare muscles glistening with sweat, Liam's mostly hidden by his shirt. If they'd been alley cats, they'd be circling each other, sizing each other up, deciding whether to make the first move, or whether it would be too dangerous to follow through.

Myka didn't want to wait. She pushed her way past Spike and marched onto the porch, evading Spike who tried to grab her.

"What did you come over for?" she asked Liam. "Seems like it's a big deal that you did, instead of calling first."

The only move Liam made was to bend his head to look down at Myka. Behind Spike, Ella made a soft sound of fear, but Liam did nothing more threatening than stare. The power of his gaze, however, made Myka want to take a step back.

She made herself not move. Horses played this power game, and Myka always made sure she won. She had to, or she couldn't do her job.

Spike, on the other hand, snarled, a low rumbling noise that held dire warning. He skimmed around Myka in one swift movement, his hand coming up to Liam's throat.

But when Spike would have closed on the other man's neck, Liam wasn't there.

Liam now stood four feet away from Spike down the porch, just out of arm's reach. Myka didn't remember seeing Liam move, but she felt the breeze of his passing touch her face.

"Easy, lad," Liam said, no fear in his voice. "I won't touch her. I respect the pride." He gave Myka another look, this one a little softer. "Besides, I know how headstrong human women can be. Trust me." The smile came back, and he tipped Myka a wink.

"You haven't answered his question," Myka said. He could keep his wink, no matter how charming he was.

Liam focused on Spike again. "I came to find out why you didn't report right away to me. Now I know. But you need to tell me what happened with Gavan."

"Ellison was there."

"Ellison didn't hear all what you said. He said Gavan moved close to you and got chatty at the last, but the ambient noise from the bar was enough to confound even Shifter hearing. Makes me think Gavan chose that spot on purpose because of that. What did he say to you?"

Spike didn't unclench, but he glanced behind him to Ella, still hovering worriedly in the foyer. "I'll be inside in a minute," he said.

Ella nodded and withdrew. Myka looked up at Spike. "Are you waiting for me to go too? Is this man talk?"

"It's Shifter talk," Liam said. "Shifter business."

"Oh, yeah?" No way Myka could stop these two men tearing each other apart if they started something, but she didn't feel easy leaving Spike alone with this guy. Whatever Spike had done, or not done, Liam was annoyed about it—dangerously annoyed.

Liam kept his gaze on Spike. "Myka, why don't you wake up the cub and take him along to meet my mate? She's human too. I think she'll like you. Ella will show you the way."

He spoke casually, but Myka knew it wasn't a suggestion. She did *not* want to go, but it was clear that they'd stand like statues until she went.

Myka made a show of nodding and turning away, but not before sending Liam a look that warned that if he tried to hurt Spike, she'd …

Well, she didn't know what she could do. She'd seen the way Spike had fought that bear-man at the Shifter fights, and knew Spike could take care of himself. And Myka could always call the police on Liam's ass if he tried anything.

Even that didn't make her feel better, but she went inside to find Ella and wake up Jordan.

*** *** ***

"Dad wanted to come over here and talk to you himself," Liam said to Spike once they were alone. "I talked him out of it. I'll take your thanks for that any time."

"What did that shithead Ellison say to you?" They were still on the porch. Hierarchy dictated that Spike should invite Liam inside, showing him trust, and politeness dictated that he should get the man a beer. But Spike remained stubbornly in place, not wanting Liam in his house.

"The shithead Ellison didn't tell me more than I've already said," Liam answered. "But you wouldn't tell him everything about Gavan, and you hightailed it home instead of talking to me. He's worried."

"He's worried I betrayed you. I didn't. I wanted to get home to my cub."

"I understand that." Liam had a cub too now, a cute little half-Shifter girl. "But I sent you to gather intel, and you didn't give me any intel."

"Nothing to say. Gavan is a crazy Feline—you know him. He thinks Shifters are losing the instincts that make us strong, that we shouldn't suppress the ones that tell us to kill." Stupid. Gavan didn't get that strength and fighting were two different things.

"You mean like at the fight club," Liam said with canny perception. "Shifters fight, but then suppress the instinct to take the fight to its natural conclusion."

"Something like that."

"You think anyone else at the fight club agrees with him?"

Spike shrugged. "No one's mentioned it."

"Aye, but you win all your fights, don't you? The Shifters you beat aren't going to be telling you they're in favor of letting it go to the death, are they? No, Gavan must just be talking shite. I'm guessing he's in favor of not suppressing instinct and letting others kill off the weak so he can move up in dominance."

"Maybe."

"He ever go to the fight club? Apart from last night?"

"Not that I've seen," Spike said.

Liam never went to the fights himself, because the fight clubs weren't sanctioned by Shiftertown leaders. Technically the matches violated both Shifter and human laws.

But Shiftertown leaders understood that their Shifters needed to blow off steam, and so looked the other way. Fight club fights also had two very strict rules. First—no killing. Second—the results of fights didn't change anything in dominance in day-to-day life. What happened at the fight club stayed at the fight club.

Spike knew, however, that the fights *did* change things, even if the changes weren't acknowledged. Hard to forget that the dominant clan member telling you what to do today had lain flattened at your feet in the ring the night before. True dominance battles didn't happen among Shifters very often, but when the next one occurred, Spike suspected there'd be many, many adjustments.

"All right, lad," Liam said, his shoulders going down a fraction, which meant he believed Spike and had decided to trust him. "Keep an eye on Gavan for me, eh? If he wants to meet again, don't say no. Get what you can out of him. If more Shifters at the fight club start thinking he's right, you tell me that too."

Spike gave him a nod. He decided not to mention that Gavan already had asked to set up a second meeting. Spike would assess the Feline one more time, without Liam breathing down his neck, and then decide what to do.

"Congratulations on your cub," Liam said, business over. He stepped forward, ready to pull Spike into an embrace.

Spike didn't want it. He'd withdrawn in a huge way since he'd turned around in the hospital room last night to see Jordan waiting for him. Right now Spike didn't want to touch anyone except Jordan, his grandmother ... and Myka.

Not mate-claimed, Liam had said, and Spike's answer had come out instantly. *Not yet.*

Which meant that something in Spike wanted it to happen, sensed it would happen, was impatient for it to happen.

Not yet. But soon.

However, Spike denying his leader a congratulatory hug would scream to Liam that Spike was challenging him. Spike didn't have time right now for the big hairy deal that would bring down on him.

Spike let his body go slack as Liam wrapped his arms around him and pulled him close. Spike put his hands on Liam's back, returning the embrace, but not as soothed as he usually was by his leader's body heat.

Male Shifters hugged each other in a different way than they hugged females. Males didn't hold back their strength from other males—the embrace contained a warning as much as acceptance.

Spike let his hands harden on Liam's back, and Liam responded by pulling Spike even closer. Spike's body read every muscle in Liam, and he knew Liam was reading him back.

Liam nuzzled Spike's cheek, tilted Spike's head forward and kissed the top of it, then released him.

"Come on," Liam said. "Take me to meet your little one."

*** *** ***

Kim Fraser, Liam's mate, greeted Myka with enthusiasm, gave her a big hug, and introduced her around.

"Don't mind the touchy-feely," Kim said. "You'll get used to it. It's a Shifter thing. Took me a while to learn, but I'm liking it now."

Kim lifted her dark-haired baby from her outdoor playpen, and little Katriona regarded Myka and Jordan with great interest. Jordan, held by Ella, reached out and touched Katriona's silky hair, and Katriona cooed and kicked her feet.

"A mate-claim in the making, are you thinking?" A man who resembled Liam, complete with dark hair and blue eyes, came to them. "A few decades from now ... look out."

He was Sean, Liam's brother, and he had his mate with him, a slender Shifter called Andrea, who was very pregnant. About to drop, Sean said proudly, his Irish baritone as pronounced as his brother's. Sean patted Jordan on the head, grinning when Jordan growled and took a swing at him.

Myka also met Connor, Liam and Sean's nephew. Connor was twenty-one but still considered a cub. It was Connor who suggested Myka stay for lunch, and he started getting the grill ready so Sean could make his famous cheeseburgers with sautéed mushrooms and onions.

Apparently, cooking out was a common thing for Shifters, as well as inviting any friends who happened to be passing. Myka had to take a step back from the huge Ronan, who arrived with a teenaged Shifter girl and a little boy with white hair. His adopted kids, Ronan said. Ronan was a Kodiak bear, but the girl with variegated hair—Cherie—was a grizzly, the boy Olaf a polar bear cub.

Myka watched Ronan's family as she sat down with Kim, Myka still wary of men who fostered kids. But Cherie started a spirited gossip session with Connor, and Olaf helped Sean prep the grill. Olaf was a little quieter than the others, but he grinned with Sean, relaxed and happy.

By the time Liam and Spike arrived together—walking side-by-side, Myka noted, neither letting the other get in front—the burgers were nearing completion.

A growl from Jordan made Myka look around. Jordan stood in the middle of the backyard, which was part of an unfenced green space that ran behind all the houses. Facing him was a tiny polar bear, and Jordan was snarling like crazy as he flung off the last of his clothes, already shifting and ready to attack.

Chapter Nine

Myka sprang to her feet, but the others didn't look alarmed. Olaf, the nine-year-old boy, had turned into an adorable polar bear cub. Jordan was the only one who obviously *didn't* find him adorable. Olaf watched in mild curiosity as the small jaguar kicked off the last of his clothes and launched himself at Olaf's head.

Olaf reached out a big, black-padded paw and whacked Jordan aside. Jordan did a somersault in mid-air—exactly as the full-grown Spike had done at the fight club—and charged Olaf again, coming up under the bear's throat.

Olaf blinked in surprise then howled as Jordan latched his teeth into Olaf's fur. Olaf's howl turned to rumbling snarls as he batted at Jordan with his paws, trying to dislodge him.

The family stopped laughing. Liam, Spike, and Ronan moved forward at the same time, their expressions grim. Jordan hung on, and blood started spotting Olaf's white neck.

Ronan went for Olaf, and Spike went for Jordan. Jordan writhed and fought as Spike pulled him off Olaf. Jordan's oversized feet flailed as he tried to scratch and bite his father, the jaguar cub yowling and snarling all the while.

Finally Spike leaned down to Jordan and made an animal sound—one loud beat. Jordan swung his head around in surprise, then coiled his tail around Spike's arm and subsided.

Olaf was already quiet under Ronan's big arm, his dark eyes wide. Fortunately, Jordan hadn't hurt him much, only a surface wound, which had already stopped bleeding.

Everyone went back to what they'd been doing, but Myka sensed a change. The Shifters weren't alarmed exactly—they behaved more as if they were filing away information for use at a later date. The conversations began again, Sean announced the burgers were done, and everyone ate.

Jordan was asleep again, in his wildcat form, when Spike carried him home. Liam gave Spike a look before they went, which Spike acknowledged with a nod.

"Something happened," Myka said once she, Ella, and Spike with Jordan were down the block. "When Jordan and Olaf started to fight—something made everyone stop. And not just because Olaf was bleeding."

Spike hefted Jordan higher on his shoulder. "Jordan showed dominant behavior."

"What does that mean? Is it a problem?"

Ella answered. "Our family isn't supposed to be very dominant. There's only Spike and me left. But Jordan's behavior showed that maybe we aren't as far down the food chain as everyone thinks. Jordan's acting on instinct, because he doesn't know any better, but it shows that Spike has been holding himself back all these years."

"When Jordan gets a little older, he'll seriously start fighting," Spike said. He sounded as though he didn't know what to make of that—be proud? Or worried?

Ella chuckled. "Welcome to my world. Bringing up a warrior Shifter on my own was no picnic, especially in the wild."

Spike remained silent, face betraying no emotion, or maybe that was the shadows because it was growing dark.

When they reached the house, Ella took Jordan and said she'd put him to bed. The kid was so out of it that Ella simply slung the ball of fur across her shoulder and carried him to his room.

She went because she wanted Myka and Spike to talk. Myka read that in every line of her retreating back.

Myka had been reliving the hot kiss every second since Spike had pulled her against him. The nearness of him, now that they were alone again, brought the thoughts pounding to the front of her brain.

Whatever Spike was thinking about took him to the front window to look out at the lawn that was fading to brown for the coming winter. The dragon on his back hid under his shirt, its wings snaking down his arms to flow around the jaguars coming the other way. Before he'd walked to the Morrissey house with Liam, Spike had changed clothes again, and Myka had to wonder if this time he'd put on underwear.

"I should go home," she said, surprised at her reluctance.

Spike swung around. "Why? You said you'd stay."

The vehemence in his tone made her take a step back. "I thought you meant help out when you needed someone to watch Jordan. Your grandma's here, and you're not as bad at taking care of him as I feared. I need to go to the stables tomorrow."

"But I need to go somewhere tonight."

"Oh. Where? Something for Liam?"

"Sort of for Liam." He went quiet and distant again. "Sort of not."

Myka hooked her thumbs in her front pockets. "Leaving you here today with Liam made me nervous. Why was he so mad at you? For wanting to come home to your cub?"

"For not reporting to him right away. My first loyalty is supposed to be to the Shiftertown leader, no matter what. But I've been thinking since last night ... screw that."

"Because of Jordan."

"Because of him." Spike touched his chest. "Something opened up in here when I saw him. Something ... I don't know."

"Kids are a big responsibility," Myka ventured, but she knew that wasn't what he meant.

"I want to protect him with everything I have. If that means telling Liam to piss off, then I tell him to piss off."

Myka had known Spike fewer than twenty-four hours, and she already was rearranging her ideas about him. Last night she'd been torn between worry that he wouldn't want Jordan at all and fear that he'd become so crazed about him he'd turn into a man like her stepfather.

Myka's stepfather, after her mother's death, had used the simplest means to relieve himself of his anger and pain—taking it out on Myka. He'd both wanted Myka around as a reminder of her mother, whom he'd loved, and at the same time hated having her there as a reminder of what he'd lost. Myka had needed someone to turn to in her grief, and had found that the logical person had only hurt her and made her live in fear and misery.

Spike wasn't the same person as her stepfather, and though the situations were similar, they weren't quite the same. Spike was Jordan's biological father, and he'd never known Jillian except for that fleeting night. His focus in all this was Jordan, and Jordan alone.

"Is this thing you need to do going to get Liam mad at you again?" she asked.

"Maybe." The gathering darkness sunk the living room into gloom, but Spike made no move to turn on lights. His eyes had flicked to Shifter, glowing golden in the dark. He put his hands on her shoulders. "Stay until I get back?"

"Which will be when?"

"Two, maybe three hours?"

Myka let out a breath. "All right. But I really have to get to the stables tomorrow, to stop them being sold out from under me."

Spike looked surprised, as though he hadn't realized Myka might have a life. He tightened his grip on her shoulders.

He was going to kiss her again. She should mind, she should spin away so he couldn't.

She didn't. Spike didn't kiss her either. He pulled her against him, wrapping his arms around her in a warm embrace.

Myka leaned into him, suddenly craving his touch. Comfort leached from his arms around her, and he rested his cheek on her head. She slid her hands around his waist, finding the small of his back, and giving it a little caress, the embrace returned.

Spike lifted her chin and gave her a long, warm, deep, toe-curling kiss, before he released her, swung away, opened the door into the growing autumn darkness, and was gone.

*** *** ***

Gavan met Spike in a coffee shop on the south side of Austin, one that let in Shifters. It was an old-fashioned coffee shop with a long row of booths, food that hadn't been upscaled to death, and coffee that was plain and black, though the place had conceded to put in a latte machine.

"Congratulations on your cub," Gavan said, lifting his coffee in salute.

"News gets around."

"In Shiftertowns? Are you kidding me? I also heard you didn't go straight to Liam and rat me out."

Spike twined his scarred hands on the table. "Had things to do."

"That's what I like about you, Spike. You don't complicate things. Which is good, because I need you to keep it simple."

Spike waited. He took a sip of his coffee, which wasn't bad but wasn't great. He wouldn't hold out much hope for the lattes, even if he drank them.

"Doesn't really matter if you run from me to Liam, though," Gavan said. "I'm thinking your instincts are going to help me no matter what, but I like to hedge my bets."

Any other time Spike would wait in seeming patience for the man to get to the point, but the thought of Myka waiting back at the house for him, watching over Jordan, the new miracle in his life, made him jumpy.

"What is this thing you want me to do?"

Gavan looked surprised at the question, but he shrugged. "Nothing you don't usually do. Win fights." Gavan sipped his coffee, made a face, and set the cup down again. "I'm going soft too. I've started liking premium blends." He pushed the cup away. "That's it, my friend. Just keep on winning fights."

"How would that help you? Are you running a betting ring on me?"

Gavan gave him a smile. The smile made him look a little less ugly, but only a little. "Like we talked about earlier today, based on strength, you should be at the top of your clan, should be vying for a leadership position in Shiftertown. But because your family is here on Morrissey charity, you're pushed aside. And yet, you walk into that fight club and win every match. People love you."

"They love me because they win wagers."

"That's only part of it. The Shifters, they admire you, they cheer for you, they want you to win. You're the kind of hero everyone loves—the underdog with amazing ability who rises to the top."

Spike went silent. True, he liked hearing the roar of approval when he walked into the ring, the cushion of sound that kept him strong against the toughest opponent. Spike tasted triumph when he threw down the huge wolves, wildcats, and most of all, the bears that dared come up against him.

He was powerful, and he knew it. The fights confirmed it, as Gavan said. If they were still in the wild, Spike would have been high in the hierarchy by now, if not at the top.

He unlaced his fingers and studied them, as though Gavan had given him something new and difficult to think about. "Dominance isn't only about strength," he said.

"No, but strength is a start. I'll be arranging certain matches at the fight club Saturday night. You win them, and I'll reward you."

"With what?"

Gavan's shoulders rose. "Whatever you want. Eventually, I want you working with me. Like I said, you're wasted in the Austin Shiftertown. Fergus at least used you a little better. You should be second-in-command by now. An enforcer."

"Liam's brother is his second. In a close race with their dad."

"Liam's brother is the Guardian and shouldn't be used as his second. And by rights, their dad should be dead."

In the wild, Dylan Morrissey, Liam's father, certainly would have been dead. But Liam had shown him mercy. For the first time in Shifter history, the old clan leader was allowed to live out his life instead of being killed or driven into the wilderness by the newer, younger leader. Civilized life in Shiftertown was changing everything.

"The point is," Gavan said, "In Shiftertowns, the leadership is all messed up. Why should one Feline clan, the Morrisseys, rule? That was an arbitrary decision by the humans. Why is Liam at the head of the Austin Shiftertown? Why was it Dylan before him? You and me know far more about what goes on in both Austin and San Antonio than anyone else. The leaders pretend they're on top of things, but we do all the grunt work."

"Does your Shiftertown leader agree with you?" Spike asked.

Gavan laughed. "Would I be talking to you if he did?"

The leader of the San Antonio Shiftertown these days was a Lupine, who had been head of the highest ranking Lupine clan there. Though Gavan had stayed on as the Lupine's tracker, no one in Gavan's family had any real power, which, Spike thought, must be at the heart of the matter.

"So you want me to fight?" Spike asked.

"Yep. Fight and win. That's it."

Spike reached for his coffee and took another sip. "Who am I fighting?"

"You worry about that when you step into the ring. I'm putting a lot of money on you, which should tell you I'm not concerned about you losing."

"And you don't care if I tell Liam all this?"

Gavan opened his hands. "It's your choice. It's not against the rules for me to talk to you about the fights, and to tell you I think you're a winner. Whether you decide to use your skills to move up the hierarchy is your business. But if I'm ever in a position to make you my enforcer, my second—and I'm not saying I will be—you'll be hearing from me."

Spike folded his hands around his cup and studied the liquid inside. Let Gavan think him slow instead, while in truth Spike's thoughts were chasing each other around like Jordan chasing himself around Spike's house. Gavan was trying to be subtle, but he'd always been about as subtle as a leopard with square spots.

Ambitious Shifters weren't hard to find—it was natural to try to move up in the hierarchy. Better to be dominant than have to let others kick your ass all the time. Even Jordan, young as he was, had started trying to establish his position.

Spike took another sip of coffee. "Win the fights," he repeated. "What if I can't? What if I'm up against a Shifter who happens to be better than me?" Didn't happen often, but it happened.

Gavan's affable look remained, but his eyes lost all warmth, his false friendliness vanishing. "You'll win, Spike. Losing isn't an option."

"But if I do?"

"Make damn sure you don't."

Meaning that if Spike screwed up whatever Gavan had planned, Gavan would take restitution.

Two days ago, Spike wouldn't have cared much. He'd do what he wanted and tell Gavan to go screw himself. Today, he had much more to lose. Jordan. Myka. Life suddenly had possibilities, ones he didn't want to miss.

When Spike looked up from his coffee again, he let none of this show in his eyes. "Sounds simple. I usually win anyway."

Gavan relaxed a fraction. "Good then. Saturday night is the next fight club. See you then. In the meantime, go spend time with your cub. I hear he's a handful."

"He's fine," Spike said, letting the growl enter his voice.

Gavan chuckled. "Good for you."

He reached across the table to clasp Spike's shoulder. Spike's every instinct told him to jerk away and rip Gavan's face off, but he made himself sit still. That fight was yet to come.

*** *** ***

Myka woke when she heard the porch swing creak.

She'd bunked down on the comfortable couch in the living room, Jordan in bed down the hall, sleeping the all-out way only kids could sleep. Meant he'd be full of energy tomorrow.

Myka rose and peeked out the living room window to see Spike sitting alone on the swing, moonlight slanting across the boards of the porch. The ticking clock next to the sofa told her it was midnight.

She opened the door quietly and stepped out onto the porch.

Spike didn't look up at her. He'd know she was there, because he was Shifter, and he'd hear and scent her. Myka crept across the porch and sat down beside him.

Why did she like being so close to him? His body heat slid across her skin, soothing her. She was supposed to not trust him, but her fears had started eroding the minute she'd seen him rescue Jordan from that tree.

"You all right?" she asked, keeping her voice hushed.

Spike gazed out across the porch railing to the silent house on the other side of the street. "When you look at me, Myka, what do you think?"

"What?" She moved her gaze up and down his body. "What do you mean?"

"What do you see?" Spike turned his head and looked at her, his Shifter eyes once again tinged with luminescent gold. "When you saw me last night, for the first time, what did you see in me?"

Chapter Ten

No question. "I saw a fighter," she said. "A jaguar kicking a bear's ass. Then you turned into a powerful man covered in blood. Scary as hell."

"You walked right up to me and handed me a bottle of water."

"Took all my courage to do it. I had to pretend you were a horse."

The remote look fled. Spike blinked. "A *horse*? What the fuck?"

"Don't get your ego into a big twist. I have to work with difficult horses sometimes. Mean shits—the stallions can be tricky, but some mares ... Man, you don't want to get on their bad sides. Geldings are the easiest to work with."

"Don't even look at me and say *gelding*."

"Calm down." Myka grinned and held up her hands. "See? No scalpel, no anesthetic. What I meant was, when I have to approach a horse that's dangerous, I have to walk right up to him like I'm not afraid. They sense your fear and use it against you. You have to be head of the herd and let them know you're not going to take their shit."

Spike's tension didn't ease. "You have to show you're dominant."

"Exactly. Just because I'm five-foot-two and they outweigh me about ten times doesn't make any difference."

"Huh. You'd make a good Shifter."

"I figured, if it worked with horses, it might work with Shifters. The difference is that Shifters can think like humans do, so that makes you way more dangerous."

"So, I'm smarter than a horse," Spike said dryly. "Thanks."

Myka shrugged. "It's the way I think."

His eyes glinted. "How long did it take you to figure out I was smarter than a horse?"

"Mmm … Couple minutes?"

"Dumb-ass fighter, that's Spike."

Myka put her hand on his thigh. "I was teasing."

"I know."

His voice gentled again, and Spike put his hand over hers. The warmth of him slid through her body like a soft summer night.

"It's what Gavan sees," Spike said after a time. "Even what Liam sees."

"Who's Gavan?"

"Asshole who wants me to turn on Liam and go work for him." Spike lifted his hand from hers and stretched his arm along the back of the swing.

"Gavan didn't come out and say it, but that's what he wants."

"Is this something you want to do?"

"It doesn't work that way. I'm a *tracker*. Means I don't quit when I'm bored."

"Hey, I'm new to Shifters. Don't bite me."

Spike slid his arm off the top of the swing to enclose her in the circle of it. Myka had a sudden, giddy vision of Spike leaning down and nipping her neck, showing her how Shifters bit, but he only caressed her shoulder.

"Trackers are top fighters of the clans," he said. "They're chosen by the leader, and they stick with that leader forever, and with the next Shifter who ousts that leader. Trackers are inherited."

"And Liam inherited you?"

Spike traced another circle around her bare shoulder. "Yeah, from a Shifter called Fergus after Liam ousted him. I haven't worked for Liam very long, 'bout a year now. That's why I say he doesn't really know me. Hasn't had time yet, and he doesn't completely trust me."

"But you're pledged to Liam now, right? How can he not trust you?"

"Because when I worked for Fergus, I helped him do things against Liam and his family. Fergus was always afraid of Liam's family because he knew they had the true power in the clan. So he was always trying to hurt them. Liam says he understands that I had to do what Fergus told me, but understanding and forgiving are two different things. Gavan used to work for Fergus too. So for all Liam knows, we're cut from the same cloth."

Spike went silent again, caressing Myka's skin as though drawing comfort from it.

"If you pledged yourself to Liam," Myka said, "then there's no decision. You *can't* turn around and work for this other guy."

"It's all bullshit anyway," Spike said. "I know Gavan's stringing me along, telling me he wants me to work for him. Enforcer, my ass. He wants me to do his dirty work, then he'll be done with me."

"Then your answer's easy. Don't do it."

"Liam expects me to do his dirty work too."

"Don't do either," Myka said.

Spike's lips quirked. "It's more complicated than that. If I tell Liam I quit, every other Shifter will start thinking Liam can't hold it together. There'll be a hierarchy battle before you can say *shit*, then bloodshed and maybe death, never mind about the Collars. I think that's why Gavan keeps wanting to talk to me—to make me start thinking about my place, and wanting something better."

"Playing to your ambition and greed." Myka sighed. "I know all about that."

Spike's brows went down, his attention pulled from his own problems. "What are you talking about?"

"Stables where I train. I've spent my whole life there, first learning to ride then learning to be a trainer. It's the only place I've ever been happy. But the current owner inherited it from his dad and isn't interested in horses. He wants to sell to a developer who will plow it over and build strip malls. The owner will get a boatload of money, and we're out a place to train."

Spike watched her face fall as she spoke, and his anger stirred at this nameless, faceless owner. "Can you go to another stable? Move your horses?"

"I don't own the horses. Their owners send them to me, and I train them, show them, help sell them if that's what wanted. I'd have to find another stable willing to hire me on or rent me the space, and owners are very, very picky about where they send their expensive, prize-winning horses. Me and the other trainers are trying to buy the place ourselves, but the price is too high. A corporation can cough up much more than underpaid trainers."

"How high?"

"Seven figures." Myka sighed again. "That's why I have to go home. Tomorrow we're going to meet with the owner and offer him at least a down payment if he'll reconsider selling to us. Then try to get a loan for the rest."

"Mmm."

"I know, not as exciting as Shifter fights or chasing Jordan around, but it's important, and I have to get some real sleep so I can be coherent at the meeting."

Spike didn't want her to go. He relaxed around Myka, opening up like he'd never opened up to anyone, and he liked that she was opening up to him. She listened to him—really listened. Then she thought about what he'd said and told him her true opinion, which was screw Liam and Gavan both and do what Spike thought best for himself.

Spike closed his fingers around her shoulder, her skin like warm roses. "Will you come back tomorrow?"

Goddess, he was begging again. Myka's eyes shone in the moonlight, which turned the blue of them light and beautiful.

"To check on Jordan? Sure."

"Yeah, to check on Jordan," Spike said. *And to talk to me. I don't care what we say. I talk to you, and I feel strong.*

Spike moved his touch to her cheek, running his thumb along her jaw to turn her face to his. He closed his other arm around her, leaned down, and kissed her.

The spark of the kiss ignited his blood and tightened in his body. He stroked fingertips across the softness of her cheek, tasted the heat of her lips. Her mouth responded to his, a hunger that matched his own.

Spike slid his hand down to Myka's tank top, perfect for the day's warmth but too light now for the midnight chill. He skimmed his palm over her breast, finding her nipple tight behind the thin fabric. Spike closed two fingers around the bud, tugging.

Myka put a hand on his wrist. "No, I really have to go," she whispered.

She let out a soft moan, however, when Spike slid off the swing and to his knees, catching the tight nipple in his mouth through the fabric. Myka closed her hand around the back of his neck, fingers playing in the buzz of his hair.

Spike drew the nipple between his teeth. She would taste better without the shirt, but he was giving her time, easing her in gradually. Shifters could be rough, and Myka wouldn't be used to it.

So why did he want to be so incredibly gentle with her?

When Spike finally released her, Myka's breath was coming fast, her lips parted and moist. Spike caught that moisture on his tongue, cupped her cheek, and kissed the corner of her mouth.

"Come back tomorrow," he said.

She nodded, silent, eyes fixed on him.

Spike had to help her up out of the swing, then he walked her from the porch, his arm around her, to where she'd parked her pickup on the street. A sleek black F150, very nice.

Spike drew Myka into his arms one more time and kissed the plump sweetness of her mouth. "Promise?" he said.

"Yes." Myka rose on tiptoe to kiss him back, her lips damp and warm, small tongue darting along the seam of his mouth.

Spike guided her up into the truck. Myka landed on the seat, her fingers shaking as she slid the key into the ignition.

He shut the door for her. "Tell me how it goes tomorrow," he said through the open window.

She nodded again and started up the truck. Spike stepped back, making himself let her go.

Myka raised her hand to him, put the truck in gear, and eased away from the curb, the engine loud in the silence of the street. Myka's taillights burned red, then she turned a corner and was gone.

Spike's heart went suddenly as empty as the street.

From his vantage point, alone in the darkness, he clearly saw the smaller vehicle emerge from deeper shadows and follow in Myka's wake.

Spike didn't recognize the car. He knew all vehicles around Shiftertown—who the hell was that?

He came alert with white-hot fury. Spike snatched out his cell phone and punched numbers as he ran for his motorcycle.

"Ellison," he said when the phone clicked on the other end. "Watch my house for a while, will you?"

"What?" came Ellison's sleep-clogged voice. "Hey, a wolf needs some shuteye once in awhile."

"Just do it. I have to go, and I don't want Jordan unguarded." He hesitated, fixing his gaze on the corner where the car had disappeared. "Please."

"Whoa." Ellison came fully awake. "Did you just say *please?* Must be something bad."

"It is. Get here."

"Sure thing, friend. Want me to call Dylan too?"

"That'd be good. Thanks." Spike clicked off the phone to Ellison's startled exclamation that Spike was saying *thank you,* and started up his bike.

*** *** ***

Spike caught up to Myka and the car that followed her when they both turned out of Shiftertown. Spike rode as quietly as he could, without his headlight, until they turned onto a main thoroughfare.

Traffic was light at this hour, but in Austin, never truly gone. Spike flowed with the cars on MLK, keeping Myka's truck in sight. The car that followed was a generic sedan—every car company made a plain, inexpensive model, and Spike couldn't distinguish this one. If it had been a motorcycle, he'd have known every detail about it, but sedans were all the same to him.

Myka drove through the heart of Austin and out the other side to a neighborhood along the bluffs near Shoal Creek. She turned onto a street holding a row of modest houses and pulled into a driveway, using an automatic door opener to enter the garage.

The car halted across the street and killed its lights. Spike pulled up right behind it, leapt off the bike, and started for the car. The guy behind the wheel saw him, gunned the car, and took off down the street, tires squealing.

The noise brought Myka out of her garage. She stood in her driveway, hands on hips, exposing herself to any and all danger.

Spike killed his bike's engine and rolled it quietly across the street. Myka whirled and saw him.

"Spike, what the hell?"

Spike stopped her words with a hand on her lips. "Close that door."

Myka gaped for a second then hit the control to lower the garage door, while Spike parked his bike next to her car.

"Now are you going to tell me what's going on?" she asked, unlocking her back door.

Without a word, Spike shoved himself past her and went inside, checking the small back hall then moving on to the kitchen. He turned on no lights, using his Shifter sight to look over the house, room by room. He felt Myka close behind him, smelled her warm scent, tinged with anxiety.

Spike lowered blinds and closed curtains, checking every room and making sure every door was locked before he said that she could turn on a light. He didn't need one, but light comforted humans, so he'd heard.

Myka didn't turn on the light. "Spike, what is it? Who was in the car?"

"I didn't recognize him, but Gavan is dead meat."

"He had someone following me? What for?"

"To let me know he can have eyes on you any time he wants. I didn't like the look on his face today when I didn't immediately kiss his ass."

Myka frowned in the darkness. "What a butthole. What about Jordan? Is he okay?"

"Ellison and Dylan are on it. You haven't met Dylan, Liam's dad. No one will get past those two."

"Well, thanks for chasing the other guy away. I didn't even see him following me."

"He was good." Spike went to the window in her living room and cracked the blinds to peer out. The street remained empty, but that didn't mean Gavan didn't have Shifters sneaking around the back. "I'm staying here."

"What? Why?"

"It's either that or you come back to Shiftertown with me."

"I can't. I have that meeting tomorrow."

"That's why I'm staying here. There's more room, and you'll be comfortable in your own bed."

"Spike ..."

"Eron."

She fluttered her hands in exasperation. "If your name's Eron, why does everyone call you Spike?"

"Long story."

"We have all night."

They did. The darkness held silence and stillness. Nothing moved in the front or the back, and Spike scented no other Shifters.

Didn't mean they wouldn't return, possibly in the small hours of the morning, when Myka would be asleep and at her most vulnerable.

"My grandmother almost died when we were first moved into a Shiftertown," Spike said, looking out the window to the front yard. "She was already sick, she'd never lived anywhere but the middle of nowhere before, and living in a city with other Shifters was making her sicker. To distract her, I got a VCR and some tapes, and we started watching television shows. Over and over again. The only thing that kept her going was looking forward to getting up and sitting on the couch in front of the television with me every day. We watched the tapes and whatever was on the few channels we got until she started to recover. A couple different shows had a character called Spike, and that character was always some bad-ass dude—or thought he was a bad-ass dude. I said one day that if I were on a TV show, they'd probably call *me* Spike. Grandma thought that was funny and started calling me that, then everyone in Shiftertown picked it up." He shrugged. "It was a joke at first, but it stuck. I'm a fighter. It fits."

He delivered the story swiftly, without inflection, trying to hide the pain and fear he'd tasted every waking day and in every dream, that his grandmother would go to the Summerland and leave him alone. Spike had lost everyone in his life—mother and father, grandfather, as horrible as he'd been, cubs his mother had brought in who'd died as infants. Everyone but his grandmother, and the roundup and move to Shiftertown had started taking her away too.

He'd have done anything to save her, and watching videotapes of inane television shows and a new nickname had been a small price to pay.

Myka was watching him. In the dark, her eyes shone, and he saw a second later that they were filled with tears.

"What is it?" he asked softly, turning to her.

"I don't think anyone in the world realizes how wonderful you are."

Chapter Eleven

The words were a whisper, and every one struck Spike's heart. He stepped closer to her, right into her warmth.

"You don't have to call me Eron if you don't want to," Spike said, resting his hands on her waist. "I'm used to Spike."

"I like Eron. It's cool."

"Don't tell me … you train a horse called Eron."

"Okay, I won't tell you. Or about the one called Spike."

"You're a little shit." Spike's mouth pulled into a smile, the widest one he'd felt in a long, long time.

"A lot of people say that."

"And you smell good." Spike bent to her. "And taste good." He swept his tongue across her lips.

Outside the house, the wind started to rise. Good. Maybe a rainstorm would come up to soak any assholes spying on Myka. Or send them back home.

Spike slid his hands under the hem of her tank top. He found her flesh nice and warm, the smooth curve of her waist.

Myka's hands went to his shoulders, fingers digging in again, as though she wanted to hang on to him. Fine by Spike. He kissed her parted lips, sliding his palms up her waist to her breasts, the clingy fabric of the tank top bunching tightly over Spike's hands. He pulled the top all the way up and off, finding a tiny bra beneath it, thin like the cotton of the tank.

Shifter women didn't wear bras, and Spike had little experience undoing them. The hooks in back were tiny under his blunt fingers, evading him. He fumbled. Myka twisted one hand behind her and opened the catches for him.

The gesture of acceptance, of trust, thrust his need high. He wanted their clothes off, her skin against his, sweat on sweat.

Spike shoved the bra off and out of the way as he sought the weight of Myka's breasts. He lifted them in cupped hands, his lips finding hers. He was drowning in heat. He licked across her lips, then down her throat, wanting again the feel of her nipple in his mouth, but bare this time.

Myka lifted herself to Spike's hands, loving the friction of his callused palms. She caught his lips with hers, sweeping her tongue into his open mouth.

What am I doing? a part of her brain cried. *He's Shifter. He was* Jillian's *Shifter.* The rest of her told that part to shut up.

Myka held on to Spike's shoulders just to stay on her feet. His body came the length of hers, his firm cock behind his jeans hard against her abdomen. He was huge, and he wanted her, and Myka knew she wouldn't push him away tonight.

He caressed the breasts he held, thumbs circling her nipples.

"Myka," he whispered. "Damn."

"Something wrong?"

"You're fucking beautiful."

Her heart hammered. Spike kissed her lips then bent to her throat. His Collar gleamed on his neck as he sank to his knees, touching kisses to her skin all the way down.

"I want to kiss every inch of you," he said, breath hot on her belly. He leaned forward and licked her navel.

Myka jumped. "Yikes! I'm ticklish."

"Yeah?" Spike blew on her abdomen.

"Always have been."

Spike licked her again. "You shouldn't have told me that."

He sent her a wicked smile before he fluttered his fingers against her sides. Myka stifled a shriek, pushing at him. "No, seriously."

"I am serious." Spike wriggled the tip of his tongue over her belly to make her squeak again. "Damn serious. I want to rip off your clothes and tickle you all over."

"What if you kill me from laughing?"

"I gotta risk it."

Spike yanked open her jeans, the button popping and tinkling to the floor. The denim sagged against her hips, and Spike shoved her jeans all the way down. He kissed the thin line of pink panties he found underneath, then hooked his fingers around the elastic and pulled those down as well.

Cool night air touched Myka's bare skin, the curls between her legs already wet. Spike blew his breath there, stirring the hair, then he kissed her, right over her clit.

"Shit," she whispered.

"Tickles?" he asked. "How about this?" Spike zipped his tongue where he'd warmed her with his breath. Myka's squeak turned to a groan.

"Stop it," she said, sounding feeble, even to herself. "You have to stop it."

"No, I don't."

"I thought you came to guard my house."

"No one's getting in here without my say-so, love. I won't give a rat's ass if I'm kissing you, drinking you, or buried inside you."

"You plan to do all three of those?"

"Hell yes. Myka I need … I need *you*."

Myka's heart and body cried out for him in return. Her life had been so empty—she'd not let herself acknowledge it. She took care of other people's horses, looked after her best friend's kid, helped out her best friend's mom.

No one for her, nothing but a lonely house at the end of the day. No parents, no sisters, no brothers. No boyfriend, because the few relationships she'd started had never worked out. She'd never been able to trust a man enough to get close.

Spike wasn't a man. He was a Shifter. And he was licking her, moving his mouth to thrust his tongue into her cleft.

Yes.

Myka rose on her tiptoes, scooping him into her. His mouth was wild and wicked, tongue flickering into and out of her, whiskers burning her thighs.

Myka writhed in rhythm with his tongue, her skin flushing and going cold, her head rocking back on her neck. She was going to come right in the middle of her living room, screaming out her joy and waking her neighbors.

Myka pressed her fist to her mouth, muffling the first noises. Hot craziness started at his tongue and fired through her body, until darkness and light were the same, and nothing existed but his scalding mouth, his fingers on her thighs.

His teeth scraped her flesh. "Let it go," he growled. "Let it out."

No, I can't. Hold it in, never show weakness, never betray yourself.

He growled again, breath hot. "Come for me, Myka. I need you to come."

He closed his mouth over her again, tongue working, licking, sexing her. He was beautiful and strong, and his voice, his mouth, lips, teeth, hands, were driving her insane.

"No. *No!*" Myka ripped her fist from her mouth as the last *No* turned into a wail, and her climax reached out and embraced her. Tears leaked from her eyes as she arched to his fabulous mouth.

"What are you doing to me?" she cried.

Spike dragged his tongue up to her navel, circled it, kissed it. The gorgeous heat went away, but then he was lifting her, shoving the jeans off where they'd bunched around her feet.

"I was getting you ready," he said. Myka felt his rough, blunt, fighter's fingers between them, his jeans moving out of the way. "I needed you to come because Shifters are big, and I need you wet and open for me."

Big? How big?

Oh.

That big.

His cock bumped her, thick and wide. Spike opened her thighs around his hips, lifting her and holding her with perfect strength while he slid up and inside.

Myka's eyes went wide. Hell, he couldn't be that …

Oh, my God … it has to stop soon …

Oh, my God.

The ferocity drained from Spike's face in one instant. He looked at her with heavy-lidded eyes, the dark brown touched with gold. His lips parted, mouth softening.

"Myka …" The word came out of him on a grating exhale. "You're tight. Damn, you're tight."

Sounds of ecstasy came out of Myka's mouth and nothing else. Coherence had gone.

Spike leaned her back, and she found a cool wall behind her. Then she was aware of nothing but Spike holding her steady, hands protecting her from the hardness of the wall, his heat engulfing her. His body was so tight against hers that his strength became her strength too.

And his cock … Reaching inside her, bigger and harder than anything had a right to be, spreading her, loving her.

She was going to die. No, she was going to live, and love every second of it.

Myka wrapped her arms around Spike's beautiful body and kissed his lips. Spike smiled into the kiss, opening her mouth, slanting their lips together, deepening the kiss.

He thrust inside her in small pushes, the space too tight for much else. Each pulse made Myka moan, and Spike growled low in his throat.

Sweat dripped between them, Spike's skin slick with it. Myka glided her hands over his tatts, leaning down to lick the swirl of dragon wings across his shoulders.

Naked, entwined, the ache between her legs both beautiful and agonizing, Myka kissed him, licked him, kneaded him. She loved Spike's hair, the sharp stubble of it. She liked it against her fingertips, under her nuzzling nose, against her lips and tongue.

She was coming again, Spike's loving tearing her apart. Myka's cries rang out into the quiet living room, his growls becoming sounds of need, then shouts.

Finally he was pumping up into her, she rising and falling against the wall, sheltered and protected by his arms.

"Feel my seed," he almost snarled. "Take my seed. Myka. *Mate*."

Myka's answer was another cry, hoarse in her throat. Spike's shout mingled with hers, then his eyes glowed golden, Shifter, and heat scalded her inside and out.

Then they were falling, down, down, the rug coming up at her, but Spike was holding her, shielding her from harm. She landed on top of him, he still inside her, his eyes that wild Shifter gold.

"Mate," he said again, and he held her hard, arms across her back. "*My* mate. Myka."

His voice caressed the name, his embrace not letting her go.

Myka collapsed, her heart beating swiftly, her body both pliant and tight. She knew she should worry about that word—*mate*—but right now, the world was bliss, and she surrendered.

*** *** ***

Morning came way too soon. Myka woke in her bed, facedown near the edge, her head hanging off the pillow. The muffled windows were dim, and rain, blessed rain—they hadn't seen hardly any of it this year—pattered on the roof. Against Myka's left side was the solid strength of a male body, warmth, the scent of lovemaking.

Spike had lifted her and carried her into her bedroom after their descent to the living room floor. He'd laid her on her bed, slid himself over her, and showed he could sex her just as excitingly in the ordinary man-on-top position.

After that … ecstasy had spiraled into astonishing joy, which eased down into sleep and wicked dreams.

Myka turned over, Spike's arm remaining possessively around her. She studied his face, relaxed in sleep, the lines of tension erased.

She had a naked Shifter in her bed. One of those frightening creatures that had to be controlled with Collars, who fought with gritty violence even when they played at fighting each other.

Then again, Spike was just a man, one who worried about his son and grieved the passing of his son's mother, even though he'd barely known her.

He'd sat with his grandmother watching television shows that probably hadn't interested him to help her get well, and he'd followed Myka tonight when he worried that someone was trying to hurt her.

Tracker, he called himself. *Caretaker* was more like it.

Myka had learned a long time ago to take care of herself. She'd be dead, or in prison, or in a mental hospital if she hadn't. And yet, to surrender, if only once, to this man's strength and protectiveness was...

Peaceful. Astonishing. A taste of happiness.

Spike opened his eyes, liquid brown in the dim room. He didn't look sleepy or groggy, but perfectly alert.

"Hey," he said. He brushed back Myka's untamable hair. "You're pretty in the morning."

"Now I know you're crazy."

"You're all rumpled from making love with me. That makes you beautiful."

"Bet you say that to all the girls." Myka said it teasingly, but a sudden pain laced her heart.

He brushed back her hair again, fingertips light. "Haven't been that many girls. Not in my lifetime."

Hard to believe. Spike didn't have conventional man-prettiness, but he was sexy. Hard body, hard face, eyes that could be hot with fighting rage or warm and dark, like they were now. And his tatts. Myka had never been attracted to heavily tattooed men, especially not one as inked as Spike, but the dragon that spread across his back was graceful and beautiful, the jaguars on arms and chest as fluid. The tattoos moved with him, perfectly balanced, a part of him, not just ink on skin.

"Shifter females aren't thick on the ground," Spike said, his voice quiet. "Most are looking for a mate for life. They want someone strong in his clan, not a tracker who has to answer to others and puts his life in danger every day." He shrugged. "They can afford to be choosy."

Meaning they wouldn't choose him. Spike didn't sound angry when he said it, or sad. Just resigned.

Myka remembered his statement last evening on the porch swing—*Dumb-ass fighter, that's Spike.*

"If all they see is a dumb-ass fighter," she said, touching his face. "Then they aren't looking."

He stiffened. "Don't do that."

Myka stilled. "Don't do what?"

"Say things like that, while you look at me like that and touch me like that." He growled. "I won't let you out of this bed. Not today, not for a long, long time."

Why didn't that sound like a bad thing? She touched his face again, turning it into a caress along his sandpaper whiskers.

Spike closed strong fingers around her wrist. "You have your meeting at the stables. What time?"

Myka sighed, rolled over, and looked at the clock on her nightstand. "Shit. Now." She completed the roll, sliding out from under Spike's arm, and came up with her feet on the floor.

Spike got out behind her then closed his arms around her body. He pulled her back into him and kissed the top of her head.

They stood that way, swaying a little together, Myka closing her eyes to savor the warmth and strength of him at her back. If she could believe he'd be at her back all the time, watching over her, supporting her … her life would be as perfect as it could get.

Spike kissed her cheek then nuzzled her, hands coming up to cup her breasts. He drew both nipples gently between his fingers, and kissed her cheek again.

"Let's get you there," he said softly.

He stepped away, taking his blissful warmth with him, and gave her a little push on her butt to send her toward her bathroom. There, he proceeded to take a shower with her, soaping her entire body before they made love one more time against the tiled wall.

*** *** ***

Myka hastened into the dusty office at the stable yard, five minutes late, panting and hoping she didn't look as though she'd had fantastic sex all night and again this morning. The rain had gone, clouds breaking up. In a few hours the city would look as though no rain had fallen on it at all.

The grim faces the other four trainers turned to her when she walked in told her that they neither noticed nor cared about her wild night, nor were they having a productive meeting with the stable owner.

The bottom line, the stable owner told Myka and the other trainers, was that he needed them to come up with half a million if they wanted to make a down payment and stop him negotiating with the developers. If they thought they could get him the money within a week or so, he'd wait, but he couldn't afford to keep the stables open anymore. He needed a large influx of cash to pay his deceased father's back debts and move on to more profitable ventures.

Half a million was a ton of money, and even pooling their efforts, the other trainers, all male, said they couldn't cover it. Neither could Myka, whose savings consisted of some of her riding prizes in the past plus bonuses from owners happy that she'd helped them sell a horse for a good price.

Nowhere near enough to make a dent in five hundred grand. She could put her house up for sale, but considering the market nowadays, there was no guarantee she could sell it quickly, nor make enough even to cover what she still owed on the mortgage. All in all, a depressing meeting.

Spike waited for Myka at one of the outer corrals near her truck. He'd called his friend Ellison as soon as they'd finished showering, and Myka had heard relief in Spike's voice when Ellison reported that all had been quiet in Shiftertown. Jordan had been up early demanding breakfast, and Dylan had actually cooked for them all.

"I'll spend the rest of my life paying for *that,*" Spike had growled when he'd hung up.

Now he was leaning on the top rail of the square corral, watching the two horses inside. Both were Quarter Horses that belonged to a wealthy businessman who paid Myka to make them winners. The gelding had retreated to the far end of the corral, keeping his rump against the bars, while he watched Spike. The mare had planted herself in the middle of the corral and was giving Spike the evil eye.

"She's a queen bitch," Myka said, approaching. "Great cutting horse in the ring, when it counts, but when she knows it's just practice, she's a devil. She's put me on the ground more than a few times."

The mare glanced at Myka, dismissed her, and moved her gaze back to Spike. Her eyes were wider than usual, her nostrils flaring as she took in his Shifter scent.

Spike looked human—mostly—but the mare's little brain was telling her she should be worried. Or should she? Humans were wusses, only useful for bringing her food, grooming her, or telling her how good she was.

Spike growled. The sound was soft but floated across the corral to the pricked ears of the mare. The mare's head jerked up, eyes now ringed with white. She whirled around, kicking dirt behind her, and ran the few yards to gelding's corner to try to hide behind him.

Myka laughed. "Karma," she called to the mare. "Gets you every time."

Spike gave the horses one last growl and led Myka to her truck.

As Myka drove back to Shiftertown, Spike listened to her tale of the meeting. She tried to speak lightly, but her distress came to him through her voice, the tightening of her lips and eyes, the change in her scent.

The stables were important to her—they were her territory, Spike sensed, more than her little house was. Her house was where she slept and kept her stuff. The stables were her life.

Good thing Spike would be able to do something about that.

When they reached Shiftertown, a car that had been dogging them ever since the stables abruptly pulled around them and raced off.

Damn it to hell. "Follow him!"

Myka shot Spike a startled look but stepped on the gas. The Shifter was good, though. He darted through traffic and swung onto the busy Airport Boulevard, heading into town and toward the I-35.

"Forget it," Spike said. "Back to Shiftertown."

Myka took the next turn and went around the block without missing a beat, heading back the way they'd come. "One of Gavan's?" she asked. She gripped the wheel with tight, white-knuckled hands. "He's really serious."

"He's screwed. Drop me off at Liam's."

Phone calls were too tame for Spike's fighting blood. He needed action, to kill, to protect, and he needed it now.

Myka asked no questions but drove to the house, following his directions. She understood why he was pissed off, and through his rage, Spike knew that he'd been right about her being the mate for him.

The Morrissey house teemed with activity. Connor was in the backyard looking after Katriona, Kim already having left for her office. Sean and Andrea were in the kitchen cleaning up from breakfast—or at least Sean was cleaning up while Andrea rested her pregnant body on a chair and gave him encouragement.

Liam sat on the edge of a sagging sofa on the back porch, watching Connor set up blocks in the grass for Katriona to knock over.

Liam rose when Spike came charging up. Connor too looked up, tensing, glancing behind Spike to Myka.

"Spike," Liam said, keeping his voice neutral. "Top o' the morning to you."

"Cut the rustic Irishman crap. I want that damned Feline dead. Gavan wants to get rid of weak Shifters so bad, let's start with him. Round up the other trackers and bring Sean. We'll need the sword."

"Whoa." Liam raised his hands and fixed Spike with his leader stare. "Calm yourself, lad. What's he done?"

"What's he done? He's threatening my family to make me play his games. He had Myka followed home, then an asshole followed us this morning. If you don't want to kill him, fine. I'll do it myself."

"No you won't."

Spike's anger grated in his throat. "Why the hell not?"

"Because Gavan didn't send the Shifters after Myka," Liam said calmly. "I did."

Chapter Twelve

Feral rage made everything red.

"You sent them." The words came out harsh and staccato. "What the *fuck?*"

Sean stepped out onto the porch behind Liam, leaving Andrea inside. Connor scooped up Katriona and carried her a little way away. *Keep the females and cubs safe from Spike the dangerous fighter in case he loses it.*

"It's my job," Liam said. Sean didn't move, but his distance from Liam was perfect for backing him up. "Every human coming to Shiftertown gets checked out."

Spike knew that. Liam even had found out everything he could about Kim, his own mate, when he'd first met her. Spike had been sent on such reconnaissance missions himself.

"You didn't ask me," Spike said. "You didn't tell me. You just did it."

"You were busy."

Spike wanted to kill him. The push was there, rising in him like black mire, urging him to lock his hands around Liam's throat and lift the man off his feet.

Spike held himself back by willpower alone, a tiny part of his brain telling him to keep himself planted where he was.

But he could best Liam if he fought him. He knew it.

Looking into Liam's eyes, Spike saw that Liam knew it too.

Spike's hands curved to wildcat claws. "Back off. You stay away from my cub, and you stay away from my mate."

Liam's gaze darted to Myka, who stood behind Spike. Spike knew exactly how many paces she stood from him, exactly how long it would take him to get to her and take her to safety.

"Mate, is it?" Liam asked, looking at Spike.

"I mate-claim her. Under the light of the Father God and in front of witnesses, I claim Myka Thompson as my mate."

*** *** ***

"What?" Myka scuttled forward, her cowboy boots catching on clumps of drying grass. "What did you just say?"

Both Liam and Sean swung to her, the brothers inhaling sharply at the same time.

They might be human-shaped, but the gesture reminded Myka that Liam and Sean were predators. Like the horses that had recognized the danger in

Spike, Myka shivered with the instinctive fear of prey.

She knew that Liam and Sean smelled Spike on her, and their lovemaking, in spite of the long and somewhat involved shower she and Spike had shared.

"He's claimed you as mate, lass," Liam said after a silence. "I had the feeling he would."

"What does that mean exactly?" Myka asked, her heart beating hard.

Spike didn't look at her, keeping all his attention on Liam. "It means I want to bond with you, Myka, under sun and moon, to make you my mate for life."

"Oh."

For life. *Forever.*

Liam shot her a look of sympathy. "It's a lot to take in, I know. You can refuse the claim if you want."

Spike's snarl filled the air, and Liam snapped his gaze back to him. Myka saw other Shifters coming out of houses, sensing, hearing, smelling the confrontation. She'd witnessed violence in the fighting ring, but she knew that if violence erupted here between Liam and Spike, it would make those fights look like tussles in a kiddie pool. This would be a true fight, and it would end in blood.

"Spike's right," Myka said to Liam. "You do treat him like he's stupid as a brick."

Liam blinked. So did Sean. Spike didn't, keeping his focus on Liam.

Myka plowed on, pretending that Liam's white-blue gaze didn't make her want to run like the full-of-herself mare had run from Spike.

"He puts his ass on the line for you any time you demand it. Then when he goes home to take care of his son instead of salaaming to you, you act like you can't trust him. And *then,* you can't let him figure out on his own whether I'm dangerous to Shifters. Isn't part of his job as a tracker to do stuff like that?"

"Not when it's personal," Liam said.

"It wasn't personal at first. I was just some woman who told him, *Guess what? You're a dad.* But no, you figured he was too stupid to check out whether or not I was harmless by himself."

Sean spoke up for the first time, his rich Irish voice quiet. "She has a point, Liam."

"Of course I do." Myka bathed them both in her best glare, pretending she wasn't shaking all over. "This mate thing is between me and Spike. No one else. If you want to know who I am and all about me, come over for a beer, and I'll tell you. I'm a simple person with nothing to hide. Now if you'll excuse us, Jordan's probably wondering where his dad is."

No one said a word. Myka made herself turn her back on the double blue stare of the Morrissey brothers and walk away.

She passed Spike, who didn't look at her, and strode all the way to her pickup, not letting herself gasp for breath until she'd jumped inside and slammed the door.

*** *** ***

Spike's rage lightened and lightened until he was ready to run down the street laughing and turning handsprings. Wouldn't *that* freak out all of Shiftertown?

Liam watched in astonishment as Myka walked away from him, his alpha fury having taken one in the kisser. Sean leaned back against a porch post, hands in his pockets, and started to grin.

"Is she reminding you of anyone, Liam?" Sean asked.

"That she is," Liam said. His eyes softened from Shifter to human blue again. "I think she likes you, son," he said to Spike.

"I'm not your son." Myka's declaration might have made Spike's heart soar, but she'd been right, and Liam wasn't getting away with his shit. "Stay the hell away from Myka. I mate-claimed her. She's off limits now."

Liam raised his hands, but the gesture was anything but surrendering. "I follow the rules. I concede her to you. She's your responsibility."

That meant that if Myka did anything considered harmful to Shifters—betraying their secrets, leading an insurrection, whatever—then Spike would pay with his life.

"So be it," Spike said, using the ritual words.

Liam released him. The alpha clan leader calmed back down into his laidback persona and called out to his nephew. "It's all right, Connor. Bring back my daughter now. The bad time's over."

Spike didn't wait for good-byes, apologies, or forgiving Shifter embraces. He walked away, toward the pickup where Myka waited, the tether of the new bond between him and her pulling him all the way.

*** *** ***

Ellison and Dylan were still at the house when they reached it. Dylan, of all people, had Jordan sitting on his knee in the living room, telling him a story about Shifters of long ago.

Dylan, Liam's father, looked much like his sons, except his hair was going gray at his temples, and he had a few more lines on his face than did Liam or Sean. Other than that, no one would know he was already nearing the end of his second century.

Dylan had a stare that could tear the flesh off a disobedient Shifter. He'd been one of the first Shiftertown leaders, having to figure out how to keep three species of Shifters who'd been thrown together into close quarters from killing each other. The Austin Shifters had not only survived with his help, but thrived.

Jordan, oblivious to dominance issues for now, played with a stuffed jaguar Ella must have dragged out of the attic while he half-listened to Dylan.

Spike walked to Dylan, lifted Jordan away from him, and handed the boy to the startled Myka.

"Get out," he said to Dylan.

Ellison came out of the kitchen at top speed. "Hey, Spike. Calm yourself."

"Out," Spike repeated to Dylan. "This is my territory."

"Spike … shit." Ellison's distress plucked at him, but Dylan stood up, his gaze never leaving Spike.

"He's right," Dylan said. "I don't belong here." He didn't move, though. "Did you find out who was stalking Myka?"

"Yes. Your son."

Dylan's eyes flickered. "Liam doesn't consult me on everything he does. And I don't consult him."

Spike believed him. The flicker had been pure surprise.

Dylan didn't try to touch Spike when he walked past him, and he didn't turn his head to look at Myka or Jordan. He was acknowledging that Myka was Spike's, and sending the message that he wouldn't interfere. He'd have known as soon as Spike and Myka walked in that Spike had made the mate-claim, in any case. He'd have scented the change in Spike, smelled Spike's scent-mark on Myka.

"Take care of your cub," Dylan said, then he was gone.

"Did I hear him right?" Ellison asked. "Mate?" He looked Myka up and down, boldly, but Spike didn't feel a threat there. Ellison understood. "Aw, man, I'm too late again. A beautiful woman comes to Shiftertown, and she's mate-claimed before I even get a chance. She's even wearing shit-kickers."

Myka looked down at her pointed-toed cowboy boots, even dustier than Ellison's. "I like kicking shit."

"See? A woman after my own heart. And I have to bow out *again*."

"You do," Spike said.

Ellison flashed him a look. Behind his joking Spike saw his envy. Too many males still ended up mateless, even these days.

Ellison winked at Myka, then he came to Spike and put his hands on his shoulders. "Congratulations, man." His grip clamped down. "You deserve it."

Spike put his hands on Ellison's shoulders in return. Ellison refrained from hugging Spike, likely sensing that Spike was too volatile, turned away, chucked Jordan under the chin, and breezed out.

"Spike," Myka said. "I mean, Eron. We need to talk."

"In a sec." Spike turned away and sought the emptiness of the kitchen, pulling out his cell phone and punching in a number. "Gavan," he said, when the Feline answered. "I want to meet."

Chapter Thirteen

Myka spent the morning on the phone trying to come up with five-hundred thousand dollars. Her fellow trainers thought they might raise a hundred and fifty between them, including what Myka could add, but that was it.

Banks and investors weren't interested. Stables didn't make money. Horses ate the profits—literally. More than one lender said that to her, thinking it hilarious.

Spike still hadn't returned when it came time for Myka to leave for Jillian's funeral. She asked Ellison to come back and help Ella with Jordan, even though she thought Jordan was probably safe enough with only his grandmother. Myka was angry at Liam for going behind Spike's back to spy on her, but she didn't think the man would harm Jordan.

She agreed with Spike about not taking Jordan to the funeral. Jordan seemed to understand, with perception a human child might not have, that his mother had been beyond saving. Jordan kept mentioning the Summerland, saying he was glad his mom was safe there.

Myka didn't want to upset his new equilibrium by taking him to a funeral home with grieving adults. Again, Jordan seemed to understand, and told Myka to tell his mom he loved her.

At the funeral, Sharon was surrounded by her immediate family, who rallied around to comfort her. Sharon told Myka she was getting by all right, and some tension left her when Myka said she thought Jordan would be fine living with his father.

The funeral was as sad as Myka had thought it would be. But she was glad she had the chance to say a good-bye to her friend, the fun-loving young woman who'd lived hard and died too quickly.

Afterward, Myka drove back to Spike's house. His Shifter neighbors up and down the street watched her return, knowing something had changed between her and Spike. A few raised hands in greeting; many simply watched.

Myka sensed the change in herself as well. Her body felt different—stronger somehow. Her thoughts were restless, and a warm ache spread from her chest to twine her entire body.

Ellison reported that Jordan had wanted to talk a little bit about his mother, but he'd enjoyed having Ellison turn into a wolf so he could ride on Ellison's back. He was now sleeping off the excitement of that adventure.

"Y'all need to teach him the difference between *wolf* and *doggie,"* Ellison said as he put on his hat to leave. "Hurt's a wolf's pride."

Ella laughed at him and told him to get on home. Myka was too restless to talk and paced out on the porch, waiting for Spike.

The ache in Myka's heart eased as soon as Spike's motorcycle rounded the corner a little bit later. Jordan was still asleep, and Myka met Spike in the driveway as he swung off his bike, dusty and grim.

Spike slid one arm around her, touched her chin, and pressed a firm kiss to her lips. He smelled of dust and the road, sweat and musk.

"I'm glad you're here," he said.

A simple statement, but one that turned the ache to sweet delight.

Spike parked his bike and went inside with her, his arm firm around her waist. "Will you stay here tonight? I'll make sure Ellison or Ronan is here to protect you and Jordan."

Her ease dissolved into alarm. "Where will you be?"

"Fight club."

Myka stopped. Spike's face had hardened again, his expression one of a man who'd made a tough decision but was determined to carry it through.

"What are you going to do?" Myka asked softly.

"Give Gavan what he wants."

Spike turned away, heading for the stairs. Myka mounted the staircase behind him, following him into his bedroom at the top of the stairs. The room was cleaner than a bachelor bedroom had a right to be, but he did have an extra pair of boots lying on the floor and a few dirty clothes piled in a chair.

"What do you mean?" Myka asked, closing the door behind them. The room was warm from the afternoon sun beating on the roof.

"I mean I'm going to fight who he wants me to fight and win."

"I'm going with you," Myka said.

Spike stripped off his shirt and headed for the closet, the dragon on his back moving with him. "You'll be safer here."

"I don't care. If this mate thing means I have to do everything you say, then forget it."

Spike turned and frowned at her. "It doesn't."

"Okay, then. I'm going."

Spike rummaged for a clean shirt. "Being my mate means I keep you safe, no matter what. So I want you here."

"I went to the fight club before, remember? From what I understand, no one's allowed to fight outside the ring, or do anything that will disturb the Shifter pecking order."

"Nope."

"So I'd be safe there. Because it's neutral ground."

Spike came out of the closet, his expression grim. "Not necessarily."

"You mean because of Gavan?"

"Yep."

"He's not asking you to kill anyone, is he?"

"Nope."

Myka put her hands on her hips. "You have a limited vocabulary, Spike, you know that?"

"Fighters do." Spike pulled a black shirt on over his head and unfolded its Harley logo down his chest.

"You're more than just a fighter."

"I know that."

"Well, I want to be more than a fighter's girlfriend. What does Gavan want you to do? Explain. I'll get it."

Spike let out a sigh, letting go of his stubborn, cryptic look. "He wants me to win fights against strategic targets. He believes that will weaken these Shifters in everyone's mind, so when he challenges them for dominance, they'll already know they weren't as strong as they thought they were, and give him a better chance. Dominance isn't only about strength—it's about convincing others you can best them without it having to come to a fight. He's offered to let me become his champion, so I get to be right there next to him when he takes over—after I help him take over. He'll be leader of his Shiftertown, and I'll be his second and his enforcer."

Myka listened in silence, her alarm building. Spike turned to a small, square mirror on the wall and ran a hand over the stubble on his face. "To hell with shaving. I'll just be shifting."

"It can't be that simple, can it?" Myka asked.

"Not shaving? Easy for me."

"I know you know what I mean. It can't be as simple as you winning a bunch of fights, and Gavan taking over."

"Nope."

Myka fell silent again. She knew good and well that Spike wouldn't simply give in to Gavan and do whatever he wanted. She also knew he was angry at Liam and wasn't about to crawl over there giving him Gavan on a platter. Spike was up to something underhanded.

"Let me help," she said.

"Shifter shit is dangerous, Myka."

"I know. But aren't I going to be your mate? Or whatever that means? I think you'd better explain that part to me."

Spike came to her, his eyes taking on the golden hue, his big hands closing around her arms. "It means the mate of my heart. You to me, me to you, one. Under the light of the Mother Goddess, the moon, and the Father God, the sun, you'll join with me. We'll share our lives, and no longer be separate, apart." His fingers bit down. "The mate-claim means all other males have to back off. No one will hurt you or even touch you without going through me. I keep you safe, and if you accept my mate-claim, then we bind. For always."

His face was set, eyes on her. To be with this man—this strange, crazy, wild but tender man ... Myka wasn't sure whether to be terrified or drown in hope.

Spike touched his forehead to hers, his hands shaking on her shoulders. "I don't want you to promise now," he said. "Let me finish with Gavan first. Then I'll convince you to be mine."

Myka let her arms drift around him, clasping his warm back. "How are you planning to do that? Convince me, I mean?"

Spike lowered his head and nipped her lips. "I can think of a lot of ways. But you're so strong. I've never met a woman as strong as you."

"Shifter women have to be stronger than human ones."

He touched her chest, flattening his hand between her breasts. "You have strength of heart. You have the strength of a survivor." He kissed her lips again, his mouth hot. "I want more than survival, and so do you. I say we come together—and *live.*"

Myka's heart beat faster. "Yes."

Spike touched the corners of her lips, opening her to him, slanting his mouth over hers. His tongue swept inside, heat and goodness, strength and caring. This man had so much caring in him, and it came to her through his touch.

Myka leaned into him. Spike let the kiss turn hard, his hands moving down to her breasts, teasing the nipples through her shirt.

"Myka," he said, savoring her name. "Let me do what I need to do. And then … He kissed her throat, licked her neck. "Then we'll talk."

"Fine by me." Myka kissed his chin, loving the rough feel of the unshaved whiskers. "But you still haven't told me what you plan to do." She tightened her arms around him. "I'm not letting you out of this room until you do."

Spike slanted her a wicked grin. "I was right. You *are* a little shit." Then he kissed her again, lowered his voice, and told her.

Myka started smiling long before he finished. "No way am I staying behind and missing this. I want to help. Tell me what I can do."

*** *** ***

The night was fully dark by the time Myka and Spike pulled up to the gigantic abandoned hay barn that housed the Shifter fight club. Spike climbed out of the truck to look around before he'd let Myka out, inhaling the air unclogged by city smells.

The rain that had graced them last night was long gone, the sky clear and thick with stars. Out here, away from the towns, the remoter constellations were visible, clustering in faint smudges of white.

Tonight's matches must have been broadcast far and wide, because the dirt around the barn was packed with vehicles—cars, pickups, motorcycles. Shifters and humans mingled in the makeshift parking lot, either walking purposefully or strolling leisurely toward the barn. Those who saw Spike lifted hands, called out greetings, or told him he'd better kick some ass because they had a lot riding on him.

They didn't know the half of it.

Spike had called in favors tonight. He'd asked Ronan and Nate to watch over the house and Jordan—Ronan because the bear was huge, formidable, and trustworthy, and Nate because he knew Gavan and could anticipate the kinds of things he'd pull. The Morrissey family was not to so much as set foot on the porch until everything was settled. Ronan and Nate, though they both worked for Liam too, understood.

A good chunk of the Morrissey family was here tonight anyway. Sean had come with Ellison to watch, Connor tagging along with them. Dylan was a regular fighter, already gearing up for his first match in the far ring, and his mate Glory had come to watch him.

Spike didn't see Gavan yet, but there was no doubt he'd be there. He wasn't one to put plans in motion from afar. He liked to sniff around, which meant he often got in his own way. So much the better.

Myka was excited, all smiles, easily laughing. The Shifters would think she was keyed up and turned on to watch her mate-to-be fight, and didn't Spike want that to be true? Myka ready to celebrate with him when he won, fuss over him if he lost? She'd put her arms around him and comfort him after a lost bout, telling him she'd like him even if he couldn't lift a bear over his head and throw him across the ring.

Spike had come to the fights every week up until now because nothing else had mattered to him. Now many other things mattered, and he saw that fighting was only something he'd been doing to fill the empty spaces in his life.

Those spaces were no longer empty. He'd found Jordan, and now Myka. Myka liked Spike the man, not Spike the fighting cat. She liked Eron.

After tonight, all would be settled. Time to start.

*** *** ***

Spike's first opponent was a Lupine from San Antonio. He was big guy with shaggy black hair, but Myka saw in his eyes that he hadn't expected to be pitted against Spike and didn't think he'd win.

Spike turned his back on the Lupine and stripped off at the side of the ring, dropping his clothes on a stool. He stood up, six-feet-six of glorious naked male, the dragon tatt embracing his back, its tail curving around his bare buttocks and left hip.

He was a beautiful man. He curled one arm around Myka, drew her to him, and gave her an open-mouthed kiss. The Shifters nearby cheered.

Myka touched Spike's face, wanting to tell him to be careful, but that seemed a silly thing to say. This was a fight. "Get him," she whispered instead.

Spike flashed her a hot smile then stepped over the circle of cinder blocks, stretching his arms over his head then shaking them out.

The refs stood between Spike and the Lupine until each nodded that he was ready. Then the refs backed away, one yelling, "Fight!"

Chapter Fourteen

The Lupine's Collar started sparking right away. Spike's emitted one lone spark, then died as he growled and ran at his opponent. The guy shifted into a giant wolf, meeting Spike with teeth and claws, and the fight was on.

Dust flew, and fur. Spike morphed into the furious half beast, his skin changing to the pelt of a jaguar.

Spike's Collar started sparking in earnest. The wolf tried to back off, but Spike let out a wild snarl and went for him. The wolf's eyes, white-gray now, filled with sudden rage, and he met Spike with a wild leap.

Myka's throat ached, and she realized she was shouting as hard as the Shifters around her. Ellison had taken off his hat, cupping it and his hand around his mouth to amplify his yells.

The wolf tore into Spike's shoulder, and blood rained down the Spike-beast's fur. Spike only got angrier. He threw the wolf off him, watched the Lupine bounce on his butt and scramble to his feet, then Spike went after him.

Myka's cell phone buzzed against her leg. She was surprised she even got reception out here, but it kept on vibrating, pulling her attention from the fight.

Spike lifted the Lupine in his half-beast arms and threw him to the ground. The Lupine landed on his back with a yelp, but rolled onto his feet yet again, coming up to face Spike.

The phone vibrated insistently. Myka tugged it free to check the number. Sharon might need something, or Ella.

The readout said *Number unknown.* Telemarketer? Wrong number? Campaign for the next election?

But something inside Myka niggled at her, telling her the call was important. She backed away from the ring, pushing through shouting and screaming Shifters, sliding through the crowd toward the barn's entrance. Once she was relatively free of the crush, she answered the phone, shouting, "Hang on. Let me get somewhere I can hear."

She walked out of the barn to the parking lot, the fight noise becoming a cushion of sound behind her. Not many Shifters lingered out here—a few groupies drank beer and speculating on the fights, sounds in the shadows telling Myka that some of the groupies were fulfilling their fondest wish.

"Hello?" she called into the phone. "Who is this?"

"Ronan." His voice was so weak and ragged with pain that Myka came alert.

"You all right? What happened?"

"Nate happened. Has Jordan and Ella."

"What?" Myka shrieked into the phone. "What do you mean, *has them*?"

"What the hell do you think I mean? Tell Spike."

"How did he get them away from you? You're a gigantic bear, for crap's sake."

"He shot me." Even with the pain, Ronan's voice took a tone of irony. "You don't have to be a better fighter than a Kodiak bear if you have a gun."

"Shit. Are you all right? Did you call nine-one-one?"

"I'll be fine." His voice faded. "Tell Spike."

The phone went dead. Myka stared at it, then she swung around, ready to sprint back into the barn. She had to stop the fight.

She ran right into the tall form of a Shifter. The man was as big as Spike and as lithe, his hair sand-colored, his eyes cold and winter gray. "I see you got my message."

Gavan. Had to be.

Myka went at him, fists balled. "You shithead! What did you do with Jordan? If you hurt him, I'll have every cop in the state after you."

"He's not hurt. He's insurance that Spike does what I want tonight. I don't trust him not to try to screw me over. That's Spike's plan, isn't it?"

Close, but Myka wasn't about to tell him that. Spike wanted to win and lose bouts tonight to put Gavan's place in the hierarchy in jeopardy, to force Gavan to have to fight for his dominance, not just count on Spike and manipulation to keep him there. Fergus had relied on manipulation too much, Spike had said, and ultimately, he'd weakened himself. When Fergus had at last had to fight in truth, he'd lost. Permanently. Spike wanted Gavan to learn the same lesson.

Gavan's eyes narrowed, understanding Myka's silence. He grabbed her by the shoulder.

She started screaming and punching at him. The groupies looked over, but they must have thought she was a groupie too, playing with her Shifter. They watched with mild interest and made no move to help her.

"Shut up," Gavan said. "I'm not doing anything to you. We'll go back inside and watch the fights."

He kept his hand around her arm, his grip light, but Myka knew he could close on her with brute strength whenever he wanted.

She went with him back inside the barn, the sharp pricks of bonfires and bright lanterns hurting her eyes.

Spike's fight was just finishing, Spike backing off and changing to human while the Lupine Shifter limped from the ring, helped by his friends. The crowd roared for Spike.

Spike snatched a towel from Ellison, wiping his face. He turned around and saw Myka with Gavan.

He stilled for one second, then he threw his towel to Ellison and came on. "Get the fuck away from her."

Gavan looked him over, inhaled in that Shifter way of testing scent, and his eyes went Shifter. "You have the mate bond."

"Damn straight I do. I want you away from her. Now."

"Spike," Myka panted, "he's got Jordan and your grandma."

Spike's gaze went hard to Gavan, sweat and blood trickling down his face. "You touched my cub?"

"He's perfectly safe. You win these fights, he goes home to his daddy."

"Screw your fights. You touched my cub. You're dead."

Gavan raised his hands in a gesture of conciliation. "If I don't make it back tonight, my men have their orders. You play nice, and everything will be all right."

Spike couldn't hear him. The world was filmed with red, his hated enemy standing in front of him, within gutting reach. The scent of Myka, like cool, fresh rain in the middle of a fetid swamp, was the only thing that kept him from giving in to the feral rage and killing Gavan on the spot.

"You don't trust me," Gavan said. "So I don't trust you."

"You're an idiot." Spike heard the words come out of his mouth, but no awareness of saying them. "You touched my cub. No Shifter will trust *you* now."

"Not true. You help me like you promised, and I'll be the one making the rules. Your cub will grow up in a more powerful position than you ever did. The son of my enforcer will get all kinds of benefits, and he'll inherit your title."

Gavan was so full of shit Spike was surprised he didn't explode. But one thing was certain—Gavan had Jordan. Gavan was smart enough to hide him well, to use him as a hostage for Spike's obedience.

And if Spike obeyed now, Gavan would do it again. And again, and again.

He saw Myka edging away, her hand on her cell phone. Gavan saw her too and towed her back. "Doesn't matter if you start a major hunt for the kid. I wasn't stupid enough to take him to my house. All you have to do is cooperate, Spike. Don't sacrifice your son for your pride."

Spike looked at Myka. She was furious, scared for Jordan, and worried for Spike.

And in the middle of Spike's terror and rage, the mate bond. Gavan had sensed it, and Spike felt it filling every space in his heart, every corner of his body. The bond stretched like a tether between himself and Myka, making them one—the only clear point in the fog of his anger.

He held on to that clarity and turned back to Gavan. "I'll do your damn fights," he said. "You give me back my son."

"That's the deal."

Gavan lied. He had to know that as soon as Jordan was safely home, Spike would be after Gavan. He'd never be safe. Gavan would have to hold on to Jordan until he broke Spike's will, or Spike died.

And maybe that had been Gavan's plan all along. To pit Spike against tougher and tougher opponents, to fight him until he was spent. The ultimate rule of the fight club was no fighting to the death, but accidents happened.

What better way to eliminate Spike than to have him go down doing the thing he was famous for doing?

Spike was a threat. He'd proved with his rage against Liam this morning—the story was probably all over South Texas by now—that Spike wasn't blindly obedient to any leader. If he didn't agree to work for Gavan undeniably, then Spike had to go down.

Myka met Spike's gaze with a worried one of her own. She must know that thoughts were whirling in Spike's head, plans on plans. He tried to send through their bond to be ready when he needed her, but the mate bond wasn't the same thing as telepathy. Spike just had to hope she'd understand.

"Next fight," Spike said, turning away.

He had one advantage. Gavan still thought Spike was stupid. In the end, that would be Gavan's biggest mistake.

*** *** ***

Spike fought and won two more bouts quickly. Those would keep Gavan appeased, make him think Spike was doing what he wanted. Spike also knew that Gavan had lined up easy fights at first. Didn't want to tire his champion too quickly.

The first real bout came when Spike stepped into the ring, tossing his towel back to Ellison, and found himself facing Dylan Morrissey.

The crowd quieted. Dylan and Spike had never fought each other before. Though Dylan had stepped down from being Shiftertown leader, he was still one of the most powerful Shifters around, and everyone knew it. Spike was the best fighter in South Texas, and everyone knew that too.

How Gavan had swung getting Dylan into the ring against him, Spike didn't know. But if Dylan went down under Spike, that would send a signal to Shiftertown that the Morrisseys could lose strength.

Out of the corner of his eye, Spike saw Connor Morrissey approach Myka. Gavan shot Connor a suspicious look then moved his focus back to the ring. Connor was a cub still, with no official place in the hierarchy as yet, which meant, in most people's opinions, he was no threat.

The crowd of Shifters and humans swarmed the ring, this the only bout going on right now. A fight between Spike and Dylan would be too intense to miss.

A wall of Shifter bodies enclosed the ring, and through that wall, Spike saw Connor tug Myka out of the way.

"Fight!" one of the refs called, then he and the other refs backed away in a hurry.

Spike slowly circled Dylan. In spite of being one of the oldest males around, Dylan was in fantastic shape, his body honed and tight. Being one of the oldest males meant he was also one of the strongest—weak males didn't make it to the beginning of their third century.

Spike tried to dredge up his anger at Liam for spying on Myka, for not trusting him. That anger would put his heart in the fight against Liam's father. But nothing overcame Spike's gnawing, crazed worry for Jordan. He needed to *finish* this and find his son.

Dylan attacked, still in human form. The two male bodies met with a beat of flesh to flesh, Dylan's hands digging into Spike's shoulders at the same time Spike dug into Dylan's.

The Shifters erupted into a roar of approval. The bets would be coming thick and fast, equally on Spike as on Dylan.

Dylan jerked Spike close, a weak move, but it put Dylan's lips next to Spike's ear. "Play it out," Dylan said.

The man backed off before Spike could respond, but he understood. Something was happening outside the ring, and Spike and Dylan needed to distract Gavan long enough for whatever it was to happen.

A spark jumped on Dylan's Collar. Only one. An answering bite dug into Spike's neck from his own Collar, and the prick of pain woke up the beast.

Spike launched himself at Dylan, shifting to his half-Shifter state on the way. Dylan's body elongated until he was half lion, half man, with a roar to go with it.

Bodies met again, teeth and claws digging, Dylan's incredible strength pressing Spike across the ring. Spike's Collar arced, electricity snapping into him, as he fought to remain inside the cinder blocks.

Dylan was holding back a little, Spike could tell, even through all the roaring and growling. Even with that, the animal inside Spike suddenly knew: *I can best him.*

He let out a long, warning snarl, and the jaguar took over.

*** *** ***

"What the hell are you doing?" Myka asked in a half-panted whisper as Connor ran with her into the darkness. "If Gavan realizes I've gone, he'll call Nate and tell him to hurt Jordan."

Connor kept a hard grip on Myka's hand and pulled her to a small white pickup that waited in the deepest shadows. "Sean's in there, slap up against Gavan, and he'll break Gavan's wrist if he makes a move. Glory's in there too. *She* might eat him." Connor grinned, opened the passenger door of the pickup, checked out that it was safe inside, and then half shoved Myka onto the seat.

"If Sean's on Gavan, isn't it over?" Myka asked as Connor jumped into the driver's side of the truck and cranked the ignition. "Tackle Gavan and make him tell you where he hid Jordan."

"Uncle Liam doesn't want to do that until we know the cub and Spike's grandmother are safe." Connor put the truck in gear and eased it down the dirt road to the bottom of the hill. "Who knows what instructions Gavan gave Nate? Like if Gavan hasn't checked in by a certain time, do something to Jordan. Or Ella. We can't risk what Nate might do on his own either." Connor growled as he swung the truck from dirt road to highway. "I've never trusted Nate. He once held me down so Fergus could beat on me. Nate was just enforcing Shifter law—I wouldn't shut up when Fergus the great leader told me to—but I kind of hold a grudge."

"How are we going to know how to find Jordan?"

"Uncle Liam is working on that," Connor said. "Liam wants you to come with us, because Jordan likes you. You can help keep him calm."

"Poor kid." Myka hung on as Connor wove through traffic at high speed. "He lost his mom, just found his dad, and now he's caught in all this."

"I know. That's why we need you. To keep him calm so he doesn't hurt himself."

Myka wasn't as optimistic that she could, but at the same time, she was glad Connor had snagged her to go along. She wanted Jordan to be all right, and the heat of her fury made her want to back Nate and Gavan into a corner and tell him what she thought.

Connor drove them to Shiftertown. Liam waited on the front porch of Spike's house, with Ronan sitting on the porch swing, a bandage across his middle, his face pale in the darkness. His mate, Elizabeth, shared the swing with him, the worry and love on her face plain to see.

"You okay?" Myka asked Ronan as she ran up to the porch.

"I've had worse," Ronan said. "Trust me." He gave Elizabeth's hand a pat. "Haven't I, Lizzie-girl?"

"Yeah, because you're an idiot." Elizabeth put her head on his shoulder, moonlight catching on the bright red streaks in her hair.

"Why didn't any of the neighbors stop Nate running off with them?" Myka demanded. She'd already learned that, in Shiftertown, everyone came outside the minute anything the least bit exciting went down.

"On fight night?" Ronan asked. "Are you kidding? Especially when they got wind that Spike was going to take on Dylan? No one's here."

Liam spoke up from the shadows. "Interesting that Gavan wants Spike to best my dad. I bet Spike can. He's a hell of a fighter. A good way of raising Spike's status in Shiftertown. Gavan is honing Spike to be his perfect weapon."

"Spike isn't a weapon," Myka snapped. "Or a tracker. He's a *person*. A Shifter person. You know what I mean."

"Aye, lass, I do. And you both were right to kick my teeth in over it. I tend to forget that Spike is more than a thug who used to work for Fergus, my rival." He stepped into the moonlight, his eyes glinting with Shifter anger. "Now let's go get Jordan."

"Where?" Myka thought about the large city of Austin, the bigger spread of San Antonio, and all the scattered towns and countryside in between. "How do we find him?"

"I have a pretty good idea where to start."

Liam headed for the small pickup Connor had driven here. Myka again got into the passenger seat while Connor climbed over the tailgate to the truck's empty bed.

Liam started the truck, looking confident, but Myka felt anything but confident. Worry and fear for Jordan, Ella, and Spike poured over her in endless waves.

To distract herself as they pulled away, she asked, "So what happened to your rival? To Fergus? He sounds like a real piece of work."

Liam shot her a sideways look and a smile, though his blue eyes flickered with remembered pain. "I wiped the floor with him, lass. And then Sean turned him to dust."

Chapter Fifteen

Liam drove south out of town and off the freeway to back highways. These were two-lane roads, on a Saturday night, in a part of Hill Country in which there was not much else to do but drink. Twice Liam had to dive for the side of the road while someone pulled out in the oncoming lane to pass and misjudged the distance.

Myka held on, her blood cold in her veins.

"Don't worry, lass," Liam said. "Almost there."

He turned off onto a long road that led into blackness. Through the open window, Myka heard the yip of coyotes, smelled dust and grass. They were a long way from the city, which was a distant glow on the horizon behind them.

Liam slowed the truck, turned off the lights, and crept along. Myka heard a soft thump behind them, and realized that Connor had dropped off the back of the truck. She craned her head to look for him, but he disappeared into the darkness.

"Where are we?" she asked, feeling the need to whisper.

"Middle of nowhere. One of Fergus's human lovers lives out here. He tucked her back here to keep her hidden from his mates."

"Mates?" Myka repeated in surprise. "Plural? Shifters can have more than one?"

"Fergus wanted to be an old-fashioned version of a clan leader, who technically is allowed to mate-claim as many females as he wants. He can either hand them out to lesser males of the clan, or keep them for himself. Fergus had two mates. Selfish when there weren't enough females to go around. He always professed to hate anything human, and then it turns out he had a human girlfriend secreted away, the hypocrite. A woman called Hannah. Anyway, apparently only Nate knew where she lived—Fergus never went anywhere without a bodyguard. Nate let slip about her a couple weeks after Fergus died. I think Nate's been seeing her himself since then, though he's never said."

Myka looked around. "And you think Nate took Jordan to her to hide?"

"It's worth a shot. Another possibility is a cabin where Fergus and the three trackers used to go to hunt and run. It's more remote, but I'm betting Gavan will figure that's the first place Spike would think of."

Liam stopped the truck and killed the engine. Around them pulsed the sounds of the night—crickets, frogs, and the coyotes in the distance. Myka shivered. Coyotes usually didn't bother people, but they did steal cats and dogs, and a small cub like Jordan might be all the same to them.

A house crouched in the darkness about twenty yards ahead on the other side of a ditch. No lights shone in the windows, and all was silent.

Liam opened the door with the faintest click. "I want you to stay here and keep out of sight." No more charming Irish brogue, just quiet seriousness. "Nate obviously has a gun. Connor and I can sneak up on him, but he might come out the front."

Myka nodded her understanding. She slid down on the seat, so she could still see but blend into the darkness.

Liam vanished. Myka tried to keep him in her focus, but he walked away into the night and was gone. The faintest rustle of grass told her he was moving toward the house.

Another rustle sounded, not as subtle. Myka saw the grass stir, caught starlight on a moving patch of fur. Connor, slinking along as a lionlike wildcat.

It was hell to sit there and wait, but Myka knew she'd be foolish to rush up to the door and bang on it, much as she wanted to. If Nate was in there, he'd either answer the door ready to shoot, or have his girlfriend hustle Jordan and Ella out the back, or both.

Myka clenched her hands. She imagined Liam and Connor circling the house, slinking low like lions stalking prey on the veldt. They'd make it to the house … and then what?

Would Liam sneak inside, grab Jordan, and run? Maybe have Nate shoot him in the back for his pains? And what if the bullet missed Liam and hit Jordan or Connor?

Myka waited until Liam and Connor had plenty of time to get into position. Then she slid across the bench seat to Liam's side of the truck and turned the key one click in the ignition.

She drew a long breath, then started pounding on the horn. The truck might be an old model and small, but it was loud. Myka flashed the lights too, pumping the brights, doing her best to make it look like a car alarm had gone off.

The door to the house burst open. No light came on, but the tall form of Nate ran outside. Myka heard the *blam* of a pistol, a tinkle of glass, and a thump as something hit the seat beside her as she dove for cover.

Another gunshot, and then sprinting footsteps and the truck listing as someone jumped into its bed. "Go!" Connor yelled, his voice muffled. *"Go!"*

Myka started up the truck, spun it around on the road, then stomped on the accelerator. She drove, skidding, back down the dirt road, pulling up to a stop before she reached the highway. No one was coming, no one chasing them.

When she halted, Connor jumped from the back and, naked, climbed into the cab, holding a wadded-up pair of jeans in one hand and a crying Jordan in the other.

Myka hauled Jordan into her arms and held him close. "It's okay, sweetie. I'm here. It's okay."

"Daddy," Jordan wailed.

"We're taking you to him," Myka said. "He's waiting for you."

Connor was jamming on his jeans. "Floor it. We need to get back to Shiftertown."

Myka peeled Jordan away from her and set him on the seat beside her, locking a seatbelt around him. "What about Liam? And Ella? We can't leave them."

"Liam is busy tearing Nate apart. Ella's there and all right, but Hannah ran off, scared to death. Liam told me to go, and also that he was going to rip you a new one."

"Diversion," Myka said. "If Nate's attention was fixed on the truck, it wouldn't be on you and Liam."

"Yeah, but you nearly scared the piss out of me. Never do that again. I'm calling Sean."

Connor had his cell phone out, and Myka pulled onto the highway. Another car was coming toward her, its headlights on high beam. Myka signaled it to switch off its brights, but the big pickup roared on toward her, not dimming the lights.

"Asshole," Myka said, squinting against the glare.

The truck neared her, its fog lights on as well, and then it swerved into her lane. Myka yelped and hit the brakes, trying to steer the pickup onto the road's tiny shoulder.

The pickup's driver also hit his brakes, and the larger truck skidded sideways right at Myka. Connor ripped the seatbelt from Jordan and hauled himself and Jordan out the door. Myka fought with her seatbelt as the large black truck came right at her.

She dove for the passenger door at the same time the other truck finally halted, inches from the door behind which Myka had been sitting.

Myka crawled out the other side of the truck, her legs watery, her stomach roiling. Connor held on to the squirming Jordan, blending into the darkness on the other side of a ditch.

Before Myka could ask if everyone inside the truck was all right, the door slammed open, and out climbed Gavan himself. He'd brought backup—three Shifters all as big as Nate and Spike, and one had a shotgun.

"You'll want to stop right there, bitch."

Great. Here Myka was, standing on the side of the highway, all alone, facing down four towering, hard-bodied, enraged Shifters. Gavan pinned her with his white-hot glare, the other three thugs ready to do violence on his behalf. What had happened to Sean and Glory sitting on him at the fight club?

"I've changed my mind," Gavan said. "Spike's dead. I thought I could trust him, that we were friends. I guess not."

"You can't kill anyone," Myka said, planting her booted feet firmly and lifting her chin. "Humans won't go for Shifters killing each other, or hurting humans. You know that."

Sounded great in theory. The human bureaus that dealt with Shifters constantly reassured the public that Shifters were contained, controlled, peaceful beings that wanted nothing more than to live in harmony with the world.

In practice, here was Gavan and his three henchmen in a half-circle around her, filling her with terror. Myka had watched Shifters fight each other, ignoring their sparking Collars or at least not letting the Collars slow them down much. Nate had shot Ronan, who'd be dead if he were human, and now Liam was somewhere teaching Nate a lesson.

At least Connor had run off with Jordan.

Gavan was sniffing the darkness. He nudged the nearest thug and pointed the direction Connor had gone. "Go get them."

Connor was much younger than these guys, and maybe he could outrun them, or get to Liam in time.

Carrying a four-year-old child through open fields? Myka shivered. *Go on, Connor.*

"Get in the truck," Gavan said to Myka.

"Don't think so," Myka said.

"Put her in," Gavan said to his second henchman.

The Shifter came for Myka. She whirled and ran a few steps before the thug grabbed her by the arms, dragging her back to the black pickup. She didn't go meekly—she kicked, bit, and punched until Gavan grabbed her around the neck.

His Collar sparked, but he didn't ease the pressure. "You give us trouble, I'll kill you. You sit still until Spike comes to find you, and I'll let you go home in one piece. You're right—I don't want trouble with humans. But I'll do what I have to do. Got it?"

"You're a fucking dickhead."

"Hey, I've been called worse by females who *like* me, sweetie. Don't write me off. Now that you're used to Shifters, you'll be begging for more."

Myka kicked him. Pain flashed through Gavan's eyes followed by rage.

Shit-kickers, indeed. Myka's boots had caps on the ends to protect her toes from horses who liked to put their feet down on hers.

"You little ..."

Gavan grabbed her and hauled off her feet so easily it made Myka sick with fear. Humans were right to be afraid of Shifters. They were strong, bred to fight. Shifters who didn't care, like Gavan, could wreak havoc.

Myka struggled against him, but she knew she'd never win a battle of strength. Her only hope was Liam, and Connor finding him to tell him what had happened.

That hope died when she heard Connor yell, and Jordan cry out. Found. *Damn it.*

Jordan, in his wildcat form, was snarling and yowling as Gavan's thug carried him across the ditch to the road.

"Where's Connor?" Myka cried.

"I put him down," the Shifter growled.

Fear sliced through her belly. "You killed him?"

"Dunno. Let me break this one's neck. He's a little shit."

"Nope," Gavan said. "Need him intact."

Gavan carried Myka to the pickup and threw her into its empty bed. Myka's breath whooshed out of her as she landed, and before she could scramble up, Gavan had slapped a pair of handcuffs around her wrists. The cuffs had been looped around a metal hook in the bottom of the truck bed, locking Myka in place.

She struggled and swore at him, but she could only hunker there, sore and breathless. Jordan fought his captor like a crazed thing, drawing blood with teeth and claws. Good for him.

"He's going to shred me!" the thug complained.

Gavan chuckled. "He's a good little fighter. When I raise him, he'll be *my* good little fighter. Hit him with the tranq and let's go."

The thug carried Jordan, who sank his teeth hard into the man's arm, to the pickup. The one who'd caught Myka rifled for something behind the seat. A syringe glittered in the lights from the truck, and the second thug punched the needle into the struggling Jordan.

Jordan stopped snarling and went limp. The four Shifters piled into the truck with Jordan, leaving Myka chained in the back, and started up the highway the way they'd come.

Chapter Sixteen

Three motorcycles hurtled out of the darkness of the highway, heading straight for the truck. Three headlights fixed on it like the eyes of a monster.

Myka, in her half-sitting position, saw them through the truck's front window, and watched Gavan's driver tense as they came on.

"Run them down," Gavan snapped. "What are they going to do?"

The driver stepped on the gas. In an eerie repeat of what had happened with Myka in the smaller pickup, the motorcycle headlights came straight on. The driver hit the accelerator. The motorcycles came faster.

At the last minute, the three bikes split around the truck, and the truck shot past them at high speed. The motorcycles spun around with a squealing of tires and a gunning of engines, and rode hard and fast after the pickup again.

The truck's back window opened and the barrel of the shotgun came out. Myka hit the bottom of the truck bed, trying to cover her ears as the gun roared.

"Got one!" the shooter announced.

Myka popped up again, craning to see. The bike closest to the back of the truck wobbled around, as though the rider had lost control. The glare of lights showed tatts all over that rider's bare torso, blood dripping down his chest and arms.

"Spike!" Myka screamed.

Spike shot toward the pickup in a burst of speed, then launched himself from the bike to the back of the truck. His skin changed to the jaguar's as he made the jump, powerful back legs propelling him. The bike spun out on the road, the other two bikers swerving to miss it.

The gun came out again. Myka rocked onto her back and kicked up with her legs, her feet catching the barrel of the shotgun and knocking it aside.

The shooter didn't drop the gun, but the waver gave Spike enough time to grab the barrel with his half-shifted hands and haul it out of the pickup's cab. The shooter came with it, his big body breaking the window.

Spike dragged the Shifter rest of the way out by the neck, his hands right around the man's Collar. Spike banged the thug's head hard against the cab then threw him out of the moving truck.

At the same time, Gavan's driver hit the brakes. Spike dropped to the bed of the truck, landing on Myka, keeping her from being slammed forward as the truck went from ninety to zero in a matter of seconds.

Spike's hot blood dripped all over Myka as he closed one huge hand around the cuffs and broke the chain from the hook. Then he was gone, leaping over the side of the truck to meet Gavan and his remaining two fighters.

Myka scrambled up, her wrists still encased in the cuffs, but at least they were free of the chain. She climbed over the truck's tailgate, landing on shaking legs. The other two motorcycles roared up, the bikers ditching their bikes and running to help.

Myka recognized Ellison, minus his cowboy hat, and Dylan, clad only in a pair of jeans, his feet bare. They both joined the fight against Gavan and his two thugs.

Myka ran past them all to the open door of the pickup. Jordan lay curled in the middle of the seat as a jaguar, sleeping soundly, his little body limp. Myka lifted him as gently as she could and cradled him against her shoulder.

She turned back to the struggle. Spike was fighting harder than he ever had in the ring, his Collar sparking wildly in the darkness. So much blood streamed down him, black in the gloom, that it looked as though his tattoos were running together and raining down his body.

Gavan fought him, the two men changing back and forth from man to beast, dust and grass flying as they hit the ground.

"You killed my cub," she heard Spike saying in a guttural voice. "You killed my cub."

"No!" Myka shouted. "Spike, he's okay."

Spike didn't hear her. He beat Gavan's head into the ground, and Gavan, white-eyed, locked his hands around Spike's throat and started to crush.

"Spike!" Myka yelled. "*Eron!* Jordan's all right. I have him."

*** *** ***

Spike heard her shouting through the haze in his brain. Since Liam's phone call to Ellison that he'd found Jordan, Spike had been running on fear and rage.

Ellison had actually stopped the fight, walking between the two combatants. No one had ever done that before. The refs had started for Ellison, then thought better of it when they found themselves confronting the wall of Dylan instead.

Sean had vanished, no one knew where, and Gavan was no longer in the hay barn. Spike had been out of the ring, grabbing his clothes and running as the refs and spectators complained behind him. Didn't matter. He had to get Jordan.

The follow-up call Dylan got that Connor had been beaten down and Jordan and Myka taken had unleashed a feral rage Spike had never known.

He'd known Myka was in the back of the truck racing toward them on the highway, feeling her presence as palpably as he felt his own skin. Getting buckshot in the chest was nothing to the pain of knowing Gavan had taken her, had hurt her, would hurt her. And the man had dared touch his cub.

He'd caught a glimpse of Jordan lying limply on the seat, fur covered in blood, and he'd ceased to think.

Now he punched Gavan's face again and again. "You killed my cub. You killed my cub."

"Eron!"

No one called him that but his mate. His beautiful mate.

"Jordan's all right. I have him!"

Spike couldn't look up to make sure this was true. But Myka said it, his mate, and he heard the relief in her voice, smelled it in her scent.

Gavan's hold on Spike loosened. Spike kept pounding, the Shifter in him wanting the death of his enemy. He'd rip off the man's head and drink his blood.

Gavan went limp. Spike went on thumping the man's head against the asphalt, claws digging into his neck. Spike's Collar was arcing, had been continually, biting hot fire down his spine, and he'd never felt it.

"You took my son. You took my *son!*"

Strong hands jerked him back. Spike fought, wild and crazed. He'd kill them all. They'd dared touch his cub, his son, his *mate*.

Her fragrance cut through his rage like rain on dry earth. She flowed around him, her warm body, her touch, her voice that wrapped his senses and didn't let go.

"Eron, it's all right. Jordan's fine. I've got him."

Myka had Jordan. She'd found him, wrapped him in her arms, protected him. The mate of his heart had rescued his cub.

Myka's small, soft hand guided Spike's to the downy fur of Jordan's belly. The connection, the three of them together, cleared Spike's vision. He blinked, finding himself lying on the pavement, one hand on his cub's sleeping body, Myka kneeling beside him.

"Mate," he whispered. "Don't leave me."

"I'm here," Myka said. She leaned to him, bathing him in her warmth, and pressed a kiss to the top of his head. "I'm here."

Pain like Spike had never felt before flooded his body, fire incandescent in his blood and along every nerve. But he kept one hand on his cub, twined his fingers through Myka's, and knew he'd never felt better in his life.

*** *** ***

"Spike's home for battered warriors," Myka said, opening the door for Liam and Kim, Kim carrying Katriona. "Welcome."

They lounged about Spike's living room—Connor, Ellison, Ella, and Jordan. Spike was stretched out on the kitchen table while Dylan picked tiny pieces of shot out of Spike's chest and legs. Myka's cry that they should take him to a hospital was met with quiet stares. Arriving at a hospital with a gunshot wound meant alerting the police, Dylan said, and Spike didn't need that.

"Shifters heal fast," Spike had croaked as he'd staggered into the house, supported by Myka and Ellison. Dylan had at least given him a shot of local anesthetic before he started.

"Where's Andrea?" Ellison asked as Liam, his face bruised and bloody, limped inside. Myka did not want to ask Liam what had happened to Nate. "Andrea and her healing juju? And Sean? What the hell happened to him?"

Liam's face split into a grin. "Andrea's a little busy. Sean's with her." The sparkle in his eyes was one of joy, and Kim smiled as hard as Liam did.

Connor leapt from the sofa. He looked worse than any of them—his face battered, one eye swollen shut, and he cradled his arm carefully across his chest—but he sprang to his feet with the vigor of youth. "Andrea's having her cub!" he shouted.

"Holy shit," Ellison said. "No wonder Sean vanished. The only thing that could make him take his eyes off Gavan would be a call like that."

"He and Andrea are at the clinic with Ronan and his entourage," Liam said. "Glory too. Waiting for the family to join them. Sorry, Spike."

Spike lifted a hand and gave Liam a weak thumb's-up gesture. "A cub coming in is way more important than me. I've only been shot."

Dylan picked out another piece with tweezers and dropped it with a *tink* into a glass bowl. "I'll catch up. He took most of the blast. If we save the pieces, we can fill up another couple cartridges."

"No thanks," Liam said. "Spike, boy-o, when you're feeling better, come on down and say hello to the next Morrissey."

"Go away," Spike said, his voice too weak. "You're hard to take when you're chipper." He held up his hand. "Tell Andrea the Goddess go with her and her cub. She's strong, Liam, and a healer. She'll be fine."

"Thanks, Spike." Liam looked somber a moment. "The Goddess go with you too. You're in good hands."

"Ouch!" Spike jumped as Dylan dug deep. "Right. Sure."

Ellison leveraged himself up, he too sporting plenty of bruises plus claw and bite marks. He leaned down and hugged Ella, who looked exhausted, then came to Myka and did the same.

"He'll be fine," Ellison said quietly to Myka as he held her. "He has you. The mate bond is an amazing thing."

"Ellison," Spike said, his voice holding the edge of a growl. "Get away from my mate, or I come off this table."

Ellison laughed, gave Myka a final squeeze, and let her go. "You're so screwed," he said to Spike. "No more mateless nights, no more bachelor days. See ya, Spike. I'm going to go guard a lady having a cub."

Myka stepped back so Ellison could go by, following the exuberant Connor, who paused long enough to give Myka a breath-stealing hug. "Guarding her?" Myka asked Kim.

Kim bounced Katriona, who was trying to eat her own fist. "It's a Shifter thing. Friends and family gather while the mother has the cub. I guess in the old days, Shifters had to guard the females against predators while they gave birth."

Made sense. Or would if Myka weren't so worried about Spike.

Connor had assured Myka as they'd driven back to town that Andrea, Sean's mate, had healing powers that would close up Spike so fast it would be like he'd never been opened. But now all seemed to think Spike would be fine without her.

Liam squeezed Myka's shoulder. "Keep an eye on him, eh?"

"Are you sure he doesn't need a hospital?"

Spike growled. "I hate hospitals."

"So do I," Myka said. She thought back to Jillian dying, the machines beeping. She didn't want to see that again. And Dylan was right—they didn't need to deal with the human police on top of everything else.

Liam squeezed Myka's shoulder again as Kim said her good-byes and breezed out. "He just needs you," Liam said softly. "The touch of a mate. Good night, kids."

He caught up to Kim on the porch, slid his arm around her waist, and kissed her lips before leading her down to the street.

The touch of a mate.

He has you. The mate bond is an amazing thing.

The room went quiet, except for the clink of shot into the bowl, and Spike's grunts of pain. Ella stood up and walked to her grandson, and Myka took her place next to Jordan on the sofa.

"Spike, I'm sorry," Ella said. "I couldn't protect him."

Spike turned his head and reached out a hand to Ella. Ella took it and clasped it to her chest.

"Hey, that was Ronan's job," Spike said. "And Nate's, the asshole. At one time I counted him my friend."

"Nate's dead," Ella said. "Liam …"

Spike closed his eyes briefly then opened them again. "The Goddess go with him. Sean wasn't there."

Dylan answered curtly. "The woman Hannah is guarding him until Sean can come."

Spike relaxed. "Thank the Goddess."

"What does that mean?" Myka asked from the sofa.

"Means Sean will be able to stick the Sword of the Guardian into him," Spike said. "Releasing his soul instead of letting it stay bound to the flesh. Nate did the unforgivable, but I wouldn't wish that on him."

Nate had died tonight, and Andrea had gone into labor. Death and life continued its cycle.

Spike swallowed. "Course I thought I'd wake up to see the end of that sword coming at *me*."

"No, son," Dylan said. "You'll hurt a little bit, but you'll be fine."

"What happens to Gavan?" Myka asked.

They'd put Gavan and his three thoroughly beaten thugs back into Gavan's pickup, then Dylan had driven them off somewhere, after loading his motorcycle into the back as well. Ellison and Liam had retrieved the other motorcycles, fitting Spike, his bike, Connor, and Myka into the white pickup. Ellison had driven the pickup back to Shiftertown, Myka squashed between the injured Shifters and holding Jordan, while Liam had followed on Ellison's motorcycle.

Now Dylan said, "Gavan didn't make it. He's waiting with Nate to go to the Summerland."

"Oh," Myka said. She wasn't sure she wanted to know whether he'd died of the wounds Spike had given him or whether Dylan had helped things along.

Dylan continued, "I laid out Gavan's boys in his front yard for anyone passing to see. Liam and I and their Shiftertown leader will deal with them. They'll find themselves so low in the hierarchy that they'll have to climb a ladder to kiss anyone's ass."

"That's it?" Myka asked. "They did help kidnap Jordan—and me—and tried to kill Spike and Connor."

"Trust me, lass, in the Shifter world, it's living death to be taken down the chain," Dylan said. "No one will trust them, no one will help them. They'll spend years upon years making amends for what they've done this night."

"Gavan's name will be cursed," Spike said, sounding satisfied, if weak. "I hope he enjoys his corner of hell with Fergus."

Dylan clinked a final ball into the bowl then put down the tweezers and swabbed Spike's chest with antiseptic. "That's it," he said to Myka. "Keep him warm, keep him clean, and he'll be fine. Now I have a grandson to help bring in."

For the first time since Myka had met him, Dylan looked lighthearted. He didn't quite smile, but the corners of his lips definitely twitched.

Dylan walked out onto the dawn-lit porch, stopped, and turned back, skewering Myka with a Shifter gaze. "We'll talk about the bullet hole in my windshield later."

"Yep," Myka said. "And in your seatback. I won't say sorry, because I'm happier with it there than inside me."

Dylan stared at her a moment longer, then gave her a nod and walked away into the night.

Myka closed the door and turned around in time to see Spike roll himself from the table to his feet. Ella caught him, ducking under his arm to steady him.

Myka went to Spike's other side. "You shouldn't be moving so soon."

"Nah, Shifters heal fast."

Spike's legs buckled then, and Ella and Myka got him to the sofa, easing him down next to Jordan.

Spike put his hand on his cub's back, and his face relaxed.

"Thank the Goddess he's all right." He looked at Myka. "Thank you, love."

Ella took a throw from another chair and tucked it around Spike. "You *rest.* And talk to Myka. I'm going to bed." Ella leaned down and kissed Spike on the forehead, resting her cheek against his unbruised one. "You two have a lot to talk about."

She straightened up, enfolded Myka in a hug, kissed her cheek, and started up the stairs, yawning as she went.

Myka lifted Jordan, sat down at Spike's side, and cradled the jaguar cub on her lap. She'd done this with Jordan many nights when Jillian had worked and then began struggling with her illness. Jordan was adorable with his too-big ears and too-big feet, tail curled around himself, his body limp.

"I think we do need to talk," Myka said to Spike.

Spike slid his bandaged and blood-stained arm around Myka's shoulders and pulled her close. That had to hurt him, but he nuzzled her hair and planted a firm kiss on the top of her head.

"I don't want to talk," Spike said. "I just want to say what I have to say." He tilted her head back so she looked into his face. "Don't go. Ever. Stay with me. Be my mate." The anguish in his eyes didn't come from the pain in his body. *"Please."*

Chapter Seventeen

Please again. The warrior who'd leapt from moving motorcycle to truck to tear apart the men taking Myka and Jordan, looked at her in longing and said, *Please.*

Myka wound her fingers through his, studying their twined hands. "This mate bond. Ellison said it was an amazing thing. What is he talking about?"

Spike lifted their clasped hands to his chest. "It means I'm bound to you, no matter what. As long as you're breathing, I'll be with you, facing the world with you." He drew her hand to his lips and kissed her fingers. "If you don't feel the bond, I'll suck it up and live with it. But I'm not sorry I have it for you."

Myka unlaced her hand from his and laid her palm against his chest. "What does it feel like?"

"Warm. Hurts." Spike smiled, which pulled at his swollen face. "Feels good. Better than sex."

Myka's eyes widened. "No way. A *male* thinks something is better than sex?"

"So you know it's good. 'Course, the mate bond's even better when we're *having* sex."

"Of course," Myka said, then she lost her smile. "I'm not Shifter. What if I can't share this mate bond?"

Spike shrugged. "I didn't think humans could before. But I've seen Liam with Kim, and Ronan with Elizabeth. It can happen."

Myka traced the tattoos on Spike's chest where the skin was still whole, the lines of a crouching jaguar. "Let me tell you what I feel. Whenever I see you coming, my heart lightens. I think, *Oh, goody, I get to be with Spike.* When I'm not with you, all I think about is you. When I see how much you care about Jordan, you make me want to cry. You're nothing at all like my stepdad, and you never will be. He was selfish and self-centered, and you're a protector. You protect everyone. Your grandmother wouldn't love you so much if you weren't so amazing. You even got your nickname doing something generous for her. And whenever I think about going back to my everyday life, without you in it, I find it hard to breathe."

A grin stretched across Spike's face as she went through this speech, so much hope in his eyes that it broke her heart. "Are you saying you like me a little?"

"I'm saying I love you."

Spike's smile died. He stilled for one heartbeat, two, then he hauled Myka into his arms and against him. Jordan spilled from Myka's lap to Spike's, but he didn't wake and didn't seem to mind.

Spike kissed her lips, his strong, masterful. "Goddess, you're the most beautiful thing I've ever found. I love *you*, Myka."

Their mouths met again, Spike's arms shaking. Myka caressed his face—gently, not wanting to hurt him.

Spike brushed her hair back from her face, his smile wider. "The touch of the mate. Heals a man."

Myka looked him over, from his purple bruises to the red pockmarks on his chest to the bandages wrapped around his arms and stomach. "I'd say you had a long way to go."

"Then you'd better keep touching me."

Myka ran her fingers lightly up his chest. "I can do this all night."

His arm tightened around her again. "That means you're staying?"

"As long as you want."

"As my mate?"

The answer was important to him. It was important to her.

Myka thought about her life of loneliness, of reaching out to Jillian and Sharon, looking for the mother she'd lost and the sister she'd never had. How losing Jillian had been losing a part of herself, how she'd been drifting, alone.

Then Spike had caught her in strong arms and drawn her into his world, his family, his community. He had a solid place in it, and now, so would Myka. With him.

"Damn right," she said.

The next kiss took her breath away. Spike was definitely improving.

After a long, long time, Myka laid her head on Spike's shoulder, happiness swamping her in sweet waves. "I am sorry about the stables, though," she said. She sighed, not wanting to think of anything that might pull her from this heavenly bubble. "That place gave me life, and hope. I love training, and I love the horses. I don't want to give that up."

"Oh, yeah," Spike said, as though remembering something. "You won't have to. I'm buying the stables."

Myka's head popped up. "What?"

"You tell the owner you can give him the five-hundred grand. Or figure out how much your other trainers can come up with and I'll put in the rest. I can't hand it over to him myself, being a Shifter, but I'll give it to you. You pretend you saved your pennies or inherited it, or something."

"But how …" Myka looked wildly around the plain but homey room, the stone fireplace, the lack of ornaments, the old television and the VCR player that had run through all those TV shows. "But Shifters …"

"Don't have anything. I know. Shifter secrets, Myka. But you're my mate now. You want the stables, you got them."

Myka stared at Spike a moment longer, then she collapsed against him again. "Wow. I'm going to have to think about all this later. When I can. For now …"

Spike drew her close. "What?"

"Keep kissing me. We need to get you well."

"I can go for that." Spike's smile was wicked as he bent to her again.

A furry body squirmed between them, and Jordan woke up with a yowl of fear and confusion. Spike caught him up between his big hands. "It's okay, little guy. I'm here. You're home."

Jordan flailed a little more, blinking sleepily. Then he came fully awake, growled again, and launched himself at Spike. He shifted as he did so, grabbing Spike around the neck and holding on.

Spike closed his eyes and held his son, the relief on his face beautiful.

Myka stoked Jordan's unruly hair. "How you doing, kid?"

"I was scared!" Jordan looked at her with huge brown eyes. "But I'm okay now. My dad came for me." Jordan gave Myka a loud, wet kiss on her cheek, gave the same to Spike, and then held on to Spike again. He turned his head on Spike's broad shoulder and gave Myka a grin, a mirror of his father's. "My dad's *awesome.*"

*** *** ***

Jordan's naming ceremony happened the next night, and Spike decided to announce at the same time that Myka had accepted his mate-claim.

Spike, his heart swelling with pride, carried Jordan to the center of the double-circle of Shifters—clan and close friends forming the inside circle, the rest of Shiftertown on the outside. Myka was right next to him, where he could reach out and touch her whenever he wanted.

Spike lifted Jordan, in his wildcat form, to the light of the half moon, which was shining mightily through the trees.

"Mother Goddess, I give you Jordan Reyes, son of Eron and Jillian."

The Shifters whooped and yelled. "Jordan Reyes!" Myka winced, the full power of Shifter voices overwhelming.

"Shift back," Spike whispered to Jordan.

Jordan gave Spike a little growl—he loved being in wildcat form—and changed slowly to a four-year-old boy with brown, black, and golden hair.

Spike lifted him again. "Mother Goddess, I give you Jordan Reyes. Watch over this child. My son."

The Shifters screamed again, and this time, Myka didn't flinch. She was learning.

"Can I be a wildcat again?" Jordan asked.

Spike kissed the top of his head. "Yep."

Jordan wriggled and shifted. Instead of struggling to get down and run, as he'd been doing all afternoon and evening, he climbed onto his father's shoulders. His claws dug through Spike's shirt into his still-healing wounds, but Spike wouldn't pull him off for the world.

"Shifters!" Spike said, taking Myka's hand and raising it high. "I give you Myka Thompson, mate of my heart."

The Morrisseys and friends yelled in response, and the rest of Shiftertown took up the cheer. Ronan punched the air, and Olaf the polar bear cub, sitting on his shoulders, imitated him. The only family missing were Sean and Andrea, staying inside their house with their brand new little one—a male they'd decided to call Kenneth Terry Dylan Morrissey. There would be another naming ceremony in Shiftertown soon.

Liam came forward and took Myka's and Spike's hands, still twined. "We welcome Myka. We'll get the mating ceremonies done as soon as there's a full moon, and some sunshine."

The Shifters erupted into more shouting, howling, cheering. Anything for a good party, and mating ceremonies led to fine sex—to celebrate fertility, of course.

Spike was all for celebrating fertility. Last night he'd been too sore and exhausted for any joyous activity, and he'd dropped off as soon as he'd stretched out on his bed. Waking up with Myka next to him had been wonderful, but then Jordan had bounced in almost immediately, and they'd had to get up and take care of the rest of life.

But there was another ritual Spike wanted to perform tonight before he went to bed with Myka, one more private.

Jillian's mother Sharon had come for the naming ceremony. Now Myka, Spike, and Jordan, with Ella and Sharon following, walked back to Spike's house.

In the backyard, Spike built a little fire in an old-fashioned round grill. Myka and Sharon had brought pictures of Jillian, and Myka had also brought a blue ribbon, one of many Jillian had won for cutting and barrel racing.

Spike closed his eyes, held his hands over the small fire, and asked the Father God and Mother Goddess to be with them. He took a photo of Jillian from Myka and fed it into the flames.

"The Goddess go with you, Jillian" he said softly.

Myka laid her photos and the ribbon on the fire. "Good-bye, my friend," she whispered.

Sharon fed in her photos, tears running down her face, too choked to say anything. Myka put her arm around Sharon and let her cry.

Jordan raised his arms for Spike to lift him. He kissed the last photo of Jillian and dropped it into the flames. "Good night, Mama."

The five of them stood gazing into the fire, safely delivering to the Summerland the young woman who'd been daughter, friend, mother. Jillian, whom Spike had barely known, had given him the most precious gift he'd ever received—his son.

"The Goddess go with you," he repeated in a whisper.

The flames started to fade. Ella put one hand on Spike's shoulder and one hand on Myka's. "You two, inside. Sharon, how about we take Jordan and go back to the party? You look like you could use a cold one."

Sharon pulled out a tissue and wiped her eyes. "Thought you'd never ask." She opened her big purse again, took out an envelope, and thrust it into Myka's hands. "I meant to give this to you at the funeral, but maybe this is a better time. Jillian wrote it to you." She glanced from her to Spike. "Read it tomorrow. For tonight, you just be happy."

Myka brushed her fingertips over the envelope. She could almost feel Jillian on the other side—she'd held this, written Myka's name on the front.

Sharon kissed Myka on the cheek and took Jordan's hand, then the two women walked away, Jordan between them. Jordan's loud voice floated back. "Connor told me Dad and Aunt Myka are going to shag tonight. Great-grandma, what's *shag* mean?"

Ella's answer was lost in another roar from the distant Shifter party.

Spike slid his arm around Myka's waist. "You all right?"

"Yeah." Myka brushed her always-untamed hair out of her face. "Can we go inside?"

Spike led her into the house, his arm around her. They went upstairs and to his bedroom without speaking, and Spike shut the door. "You want to read that now?"

Myka looked at the letter again, written on the thick blue stationery Jillian had liked. She'd found email and texting too informal, and sent her friends and family cards and letters for special occasions.

"No." Myka slid the letter into her purse. "Sharon's right. Tonight … I need you."

"I need you, Myka." The low throb in Spike's voice undid her. Myka opened her arms, and Spike came to her, enclosing her in his strength.

*** *** ***

Myka gave herself to the wildness that was Spike. He pinned her on the bed with strong arms, showing her how much better he felt by driving inside her until her shouts and his mingled in the cool air.

Spike also showed her how gentle he could be, kissing her fingertips, her lips, her skin, the touches tender and light. He licked her after that, tasting her breasts, her belly, and the heat between her legs. Myka arched under his mouth, letting herself come again in a crazy storm of pleasure.

Spike was back inside her right after that, his face softening as he felt her, eyes staying dark, beautiful brown, mouth finding hers as he spilled his seed.

After that, silence. The quiet ticking of a clock, the final creak of the mattress, the warmth of Spike along her back. Myka tumbled into a hard, spirit-soothing, sleep.

When she opened her eyes again, the room was still dark.

Spike slept, relaxed, on his stomach, his face turned to her on the pillow. He'd slid one arm across Myka in his sleep, cradling her close. Moonlight trickled through the window, sharpening the lines of Spike's tattoos at the same time it softened his face.

The moonlight also fell on Myka's purse, and the blue of the envelope sticking out of it. Myka carefully slid out from under Spike's arm, took the two steps across the room, fetched the letter, opened it, moved to the moonlight, and started to read.

Jillian's voice came to her across the divide.

I hope that while you're reading this, Myka, you're with Spike.

Don't jump in surprise – you have to know that I sent you *off to find him because I wanted you to meet him. I could have called Spike myself, or sent my mom to pick him up, or hired a cab to bring him to me. But I wanted you to know him.*

Why? Because when I first met Spike, he reminded me a lot of you – lonely and pretending not to be. When I realized I'd be leaving this life, I knew I had to let Spike find you, and you him.

Shifters are incredible beings, Myka. They have more humanity in them than humans, I think. I learned that when I hung out at Shifter bars, talking to them, getting to know them. Everyone called me a Shifter groupie, but I didn't care. Shifters worry about the same things we do – how to raise their kids, how to put food on the table, how to keep the family together.

Stay with Spike. Please. I knew him only such a brief time, but I could see something in him that was remarkable.

Besides, what better people to raise my son than my best friend and the Shifter who helped convince me that Shifters were the most amazing creatures I've ever met?

If you're wondering why I didn't tell him about Jordan right away, it was because I was scared. I didn't want to lose Jordan, and I didn't want to become a Shifter mate. Or anyone's mate, or wife. That wasn't me.

A free spirit, Mom always called me. Selfish, maybe, but you knew me. Somehow I always sensed I didn't have much time to live, and I wanted to grab as much of life as I could. Jordan was part of that life, the best part.

Now Jordan will be with his dad, which is where he belongs. And you should be with him and Spike too.

I love you, Myka. Kiss Jordan good night for me, and tell Spike thank you.

God bless.

Spike's callused fingers took the letter from Myka's hands. He read it, while Myka watched him, tears blurring her eyes.

Spike's throat moved in a swallow as he finished. He set the letter aside and enfolded Myka into his arms. "I wish I'd known her better," he said in his low voice. "The mother of my son."

Myka rested her head on his chest, loving the thump of his heart. "I can tell you all about her."

"I'd like that."

Myka tried to smile. "She was a crafty woman. Matchmaking to the last."

"I'm glad she was." Spike put his thumbs under Myka's chin. "I'm glad she brought you to me. Mate of my heart."

Myka kissed his chest, right over the place where his heart lay. "Mate of my heart," she echoed.

"I love you, Myka." Spike kissed her mouth, his lips warm with afterglow.

"I love you, Eron."

Spike's arms tightened around her at the sound of his real name, his naked body hot against hers. The jaguar tattoos moved with his embrace, as he scooped her up to him to kiss her again, this kiss tinged with wildness.

The moonlight touched them with kind light, and under that light, Spike carried Myka to the bed one more time, coming into her and surrounding her with bliss.

End

Want more Shifters?

Read on for a preview of

Mate Claimed
Shifters Unbound
Book Four

and

Pride Mates
Shifters Unbound
Book One

Plus the full text
Of the short story

Shifter Made

A Shifters Unbound
Prequel

Mate Claimed

Shifters Unbound
Book Four
by Jennifer Ashley

Chapter One

Iona smelled him long before she saw him—Eric Warden, the alpha Feline who ran the local Shiftertown, who'd decided to make half-Shifter Iona Duncan's life hell.

She loped down the desert canyon, rock grating on her paws. The Nevada night was warm though it was early winter, the sky a riot of stars, the glow of the city far behind. Out here, Iona could be what she was meant to be—a wildcat, a Feline Shifter, running free.

For some reason, Eric wanted to end that.

Catch me if you can, Feline.

Last night, after her half sister's bridal shower, Iona had stayed out until dawn with Nicole and about twenty friends—all human. They'd gone to a human bar, no Shifters allowed, thank God. They'd liberated the bar of plenty of margaritas before limping home in the light of early morning. Iona had snatched a couple hours of sleep before she'd dragged herself to work.

The frenzy of the night out followed by the hangover of the day triggered Iona's need to shift. After work, Iona had driven her red pickup out to her favorite spot in the middle of the desert, off-roading half an hour to get there. She'd barely shed her clothes before her wildcat had taken over.

And now Eric was following her.

He pounded behind her, a powerhouse Shifter, his wildcat more snow leopard than anything else. Sleek, strong, cunning. Feline Shifters were a mixture of all wildcats—lion, leopard, jaguar, cheetah, tiger, and others—but most Shifters tended toward a certain type.

Iona was mostly panther, with black fur to match the hair she had while human. Her panther was long-legged, sure-footed, and a good jumper. This was her territory, and she laughed with glee as she left Eric far behind.

She dodged across a dry wash, kicking up dust, and scrambled into the rocky crevices on the other side. She knew by scent how far she was from Area 51, a place guarded by men with SUVs and rifles. Shifters could escape their detection if they wanted to, but the other direction, east and a little north of here, was safer. Iona hopped from one sandstone ledge to the next, her paws scrabbling a little in the gravel.

She loved this. The joy of being in wild country nearly impossible for humans to reach was heady. *This is what I'm meant to be.*

Damned if Eric didn't follow right after her, faster than she'd thought he would. Iona crested the ridge at the top of the canyon and kept going.

She ran along a ledge and dropped down the other side of the ridge. Before she got to the bottom, she slunk into a shallow cave she knew was there from previous exploration. Anyone watching from the top would see only that she'd vanished.

Eric wouldn't need to see her to find her, though. He'd scent her, but why make it easy for him?

Ever since Eric had spotted her in Coolers last spring, one of the few clubs that allowed in Shifters, he'd tracked her. *Stalked her,* Iona corrected.

Damned stubborn, hotter-than-hell Shifter with the green eyes—he'd followed her when she went out at night, sometimes showing up at her house or coming after her on her runs. She'd spot him here and there throughout the day, when she went to work or ran errands or drove out to a building site. Protecting her, Eric said. Driving her insane, was more like it.

The fact that Iona was half Shifter was a deep, dark secret her mother and half sister had kept for thirty-two years. Eric's interest in her was dangerous, could expose her as Shifter, and once that happened, her happy life would be over.

But Eric's scent had triggered something in Iona from the moment he'd sat down next to her in the club's dark corner and told her he knew what Iona was. He'd smelled of sweat and the night, and a musk that had made everything in her alert and aware.

His scent was stronger now, overlaid with that of his wildcat. He was coming.

Iona flattened herself into the black shadows at the back of the cave, but Eric was at the entrance, his leopard filling the opening. She faced him, ears flat against her head, her fur rising on her neck.

Eric didn't move. Dominants didn't need to show teeth or make any noise to tell another Shifter who was in charge. You knew.

He was far larger and more powerful than a natural snow leopard, his pelt creamy white and branded with a black jagged pattern. His eyes, fixed on her, were jade green.

Iona's wildcat was more slender than Eric's but no smaller, though it would be an interesting contest to see whether she matched him in strength. The biggest difference between them, though, was that Eric wore a silver and black Collar, and Iona did not.

Eric rose on his hind legs until his head nearly touched the roof of the cave. At the same time, his fur and cat limbs flowed into human bones and flesh. In a few seconds, a man stood in the leopard's place, a tall, muscular, naked male who made Iona's heart pound.

His face was hard and square, his chocolate brown hair cut short. A black tattoo swirled around his large shoulder and trailed down his arm in a jagged line. The tattoo wasn't magical—Shifters didn't need tatts. Eric just liked it.

His green eyes saw everything. There was no escaping that gaze once it fixed on you, even across a packed dance floor in a Las Vegas club. Iona still remembered the burn of his stare across the room; Eric, the first person in Iona's life outside her family who'd looked at her and recognized her as Shifter.

Even through her worry and anger, Iona had to concede that Eric was delectable. He put to shame all the guys who'd tried last night to get her to dance with them.

What was between Eric's legs put them to shame too. The man was *hung*.

"You can't keep this up," Eric said. His voice, deep and fine, with the barest touch of Scots, had lately started invading her dreams.

Iona gave him a snarl to let him know he didn't worry her. Which was bullshit. He could take her in a heartbeat and both of them knew it.

Eric took one step forward. She crouched, waiting, letting him take another step, and another.

Once he'd cleared the entrance to the cave, Iona leapt up and sprang past him. His leopard she couldn't outrun, but she could outrun him in her animal form while he remained human. She barreled out of the cave and onto the rocks …

And found two hundred pounds of leopard on top of her, pinning her to the ledge.

How the hell did he shift that fast? Shifting took a while for Iona, and it could be painful. Eric flowed into his wildcat so smoothly it made her sick.

His growl became bad tempered as Iona struggled. His ears went flat, and he locked his teeth around her throat.

Fur protected Iona from the prick of his fangs, but she panicked. He could kill her right now, rip out her throat or slice open her belly. The panther sensed his strength—a fight with him would be tough. She couldn't get away—he was too fast.

Iona shifted. She didn't want to, but some instinct told her he wouldn't hurt her if she became a human.

She felt her claws change to fingers and toes, her pelt fade and withdraw to become human flesh.

Eric lifted his long teeth from her throat, but he didn't do anything to stop her shifting. He waited and watched until Iona became a human woman, one with a large, soft-furred snow leopard draped over her bare body.

That large, soft-furred, snow leopard suddenly became a man. One minute Iona had a big kitty lying on her, the next, a strong, naked human male pinned her to the ground.

She struggled, but Eric trapped her wrists and held them against the cold gravel. He wanted her to look away as he stared her down, but she refused to. Somehow Iona knew that if she ever did look away, she'd lose—not only now, but always.

"I told you to call me when you needed to go running," he growled.

"You follow me anyway. Why should I bother?"

"I scented you fighting the shift even as you drove away. It's getting harder, isn't it?"

Iona tried to ignore the stab of fear his words gave her. "Why can't you leave me alone? If anyone finds out I'm Shifter …"

She knew exactly what they'd do. The human Shifter bureau would slap a Collar on her without listening to her protests, strip Iona of all her rights, and keep her in quarantine before releasing her to whatever Shifter they assigned to keep her under control. Three guesses as to who that Shifter would be.

And who the hell knew what they'd do to Iona's mother, who'd kept the fact that Iona was half Shifter quiet all this time.

"I can't leave you alone. You're in my jurisdiction, my responsibility. And you're losing control, aren't you?"

Iona shivered with more than anger. His long body was hard on hers, muscles gleaming with sweat in the moonlight. Eric's living strength made the wild thing in her want to respond.

"I was hung over," she said. "I'm not like this every day."

Eric lowered his head and inhaled, his nose touching her throat. "You will be soon. Your mating need is high and getting stronger."

That need pounded through her, tried to make Iona's body rise to his. *A male, ready for you – take him!*

"What I do is none of your business," Iona managed to say. "Leave me the hell alone. My life has been fine so far without you in it."

"But I'm in it now." His voice was deep and rumbling, almost a purr. The tattoo that wound down his arm kept drawing her gaze, and she so much wanted to touch it…

For Eric's part, he was barely holding on to his self-control. Iona's scent was that of a female Feline who'd reached her fertile years, a little over thirty by human standards, a few years past cub by Shifter.

This female Feline didn't know how to control her pheromones, didn't realize she was broadcasting her availability to every Shifter male far and wide. She might as well hold up a flashing sign.

Good thing Eric was so disciplined, still mourning his mate lost long ago, so uninterested in mating. Right?

Or he'd be hard as a rock, wanting to say *to hell with it* and take her. They were alone in the middle of nowhere, and Eric was within his rights to take whatever stray adult female wandered into his territory.

He didn't necessarily have to mate-claim her. As clan leader as well as pride leader, he could father cubs on a lone female belonging to no pride or clan if he wanted to. For the good of the clan, for the strength of his pride. So he could say.

But those had been the rules in the wild. Shifters were tamer, now, civilized. Living together in a community, in harmony. *And all that crap.*

Eric's instincts said, *Screw the rules. She's unmated and unclaimed. By rights, she's fair game, and I found her. That makes her mine.*

Wouldn't that be sweet? Iona Duncan had a face that was pure Celtic, her hair black as the night sky, her eyes the light ice blue of her ancestors. Shifters had been created about the time the Nordic invaders would have been subduing Celts in northern Scotland, and some of that mixture had gotten into Iona.

Now her soft but strong body was under his, and her blue eyes held longing, oceans of it.

"Does it hurt?" Eric asked in a gentler tone.

"Having a big Shifter male resting his weight on my wrists? I'd say yes."

Eric wanted to laugh. He liked the challenge in her, liked that she wasn't cringing, timid, and submissive. Untrained, yes; terrified, no.

"I mean the mating need," Eric said. "It's rising in you, and you can't stop it. That's why you're out here, why you've been running around like a crazy thing. You want to be wild, to taste the wind. To hunt. To feel the fear in you flow to the innocent creatures out there, to make them fear *you*."

Iona stopped squirming, her eyes going still. Eric read the hunger in her, the need to find a male, to mate in wild frenzy for days. Iona wasn't stopped by a Collar. Her instincts would flow like fire. Untamed.

Eric's own need rose in response. He wanted to kiss that fire, to taste the freedom in her that was now only a memory to him.

He nuzzled the line of her hair, already knowing her scent, already familiar with it.

"I'll take care of you," he said. "You'll become part of my pride, and I'll look after you. Me and my sister and my son. We'll take care of you from now on."

Iona's glare returned. "I don't *want* to be part of your pride. They'd put that Collar on me." Her frenzied gaze went to the chain fused to Eric's neck, the Celtic knot resting on his throat. "It's painful, isn't it? When the Collar goes on?"

"Yes." Eric couldn't lie. He remembered the agony when the Collar had locked around his throat, every second of it, though it had been twenty years ago now. The Collars hurt anew whenever a Shifter's violent nature rose within him—the Collar shocked so hard it knocked said Shifter flat on his ass for a while.

"Why would you want me to experience that?" Iona asked. "You say you want to take care of me, but you want me to go through taking the Collar?"

"No, I don't." And if Eric did things right, she wouldn't have to wear a Collar, ever.

The urge to take Iona far away, to hide her somewhere from prying eyes, to protect her from the world was making him crazy. *Protect the mate* was the instinct that drove all males.

Eric caressed her wrists where he held them down. "If you don't acknowledge the Shifter, if you don't learn how to control what's going on inside you, you're going to go feral."

"Feral?" Her sable brows drew down. "What the hell does that mean?"

"It means what it sounds like. The beast in you takes over, and you forget what it is to be human, even in your human form. You'll live only to kill and to mate. You'll start resenting your family for trying to keep you home. You'll try to get away from them. You might even hurt them."

Iona looked stunned. "I'd never do that."

"You won't mean to, but you will. You can keep them safe if you learn how to be Shifter and live with Shifters. I won't let humans know anything about you until the Collar is on you, and you're ready."

"My point is that humans should never have to *know* I'm Shifter. No one's ever suspected, but they will if an asshole Shifter keeps following me around."

Eric clamped down on her wrists, at the end of his patience. "If you go feral, they might not bother Collaring you. They'll just shoot you like an animal, and your mother will go to prison for not reporting your existence. Is that really what you want?"

He felt her fear reaction, but Iona kept up her glare. "I'm half human. Won't that keep me from going feral?"

"Not necessarily. Sometimes the human side helps. Sometimes it doesn't."

"I'm not giving up my entire life to live with you in a ghetto because you say I *might* go crazy," Iona said. "I'll risk it."

Eric growled. "I can't let you go on living without protection."

Her eyes widened. "How do you plan to protect me? Abduct me and lock me in your house? What would the human police say to that?"

Taking her home and keeping her there was exactly what Eric wanted to do. At any other time, he'd simply do it. Iona was getting out of control, and she needed help.

But Shiftertown might not be the safest place for her at the moment, now that the idiot human government had decided—to save money—to shut down a northern Nevada Shiftertown and relocate all those Shifters to Eric's Shiftertown. The humans, in their ignorance, had decided that the new Shifters would simply be absorbed under Eric's leadership.

What the humans didn't understand—in spite of Eric talking himself blue to explain—was that Shifters of both Shiftertowns were used to a certain hierarchy and couldn't change it overnight. The other Shiftertown leader was being forced to step down a few rungs under Eric, which wasn't going over well, especially since that leader was a Feline-hating Lupine.

Eric at least had persuaded the humans to let him meet the other leader, Graham McNeil, face-to-face before the new Shifters moved down here. Eric had found McNeil to be a disgruntled, old-fashioned Shifter, furious that the humans were forcing him to submit to Eric's rule.

McNeil was going to be trouble. He already had been, demanding more meetings with humans without Eric, insisting that Eric's Shifters got turned out of their houses and crammed in with others so McNeil's Shifters wouldn't have to wait for the new housing to be built.

McNeil was going to challenge for leadership—Eric had known that before the man opened his mouth. McNeil's Shiftertown had been all Lupine, and his Lupines were less than thrilled to learn that they had to adapt to living with bears and Felines.

And in the middle of all this, a young, fertile female with the rising need to mate was running around loose and unprotected.

Iona struggled to sit up again. It went against Eric's every instinct to lift himself from the cushion of her body, but he did it.

She leaned against the rock wall and scraped her hair back from her face. Goddess, she was sexy, bare breasted in the moonlight, lifting midnight hair from her sharp-boned face.

Naked and beautiful, filling Eric's brain with wanting. *And* if he did this right, she might provide the answer to some of his Shiftertown problems.

"I was coming to see you tonight for a reason," Eric said. "Not just to track you down. I came to ask you to have Duncan Construction bid on the housing project to expand Shiftertown."

Iona stared at him in surprise, letting go of the hair she'd been smoothing. "Why would I want to do that?"

"Because I need someone I can trust to build these houses. Shifter houses aren't just places for Shifters to live. I need them constructed in a way that's best for Shifters. It's important."

She looked curious in spite of her caution. "What do you mean, in a way that's best for Shifters?"

Eric couldn't explain—yet. He'd have to wait before he revealed to her that Shifter houses didn't simply hold Shifter families. They held secrets of Shifter clans that humans could never know about.

Even McNeil would need to protect the secrets of his pack, probably why the man wanted to move into the existing Shifter houses—they already had the necessary spaces. Eric had planned to modify the new houses the same way he and his Shifters had modified the old houses, a little bit, over time, so the humans never realized they were doing it. But Graham's Shifters didn't have the patience, and it would be smarter to do it right away. Using Iona's company and guiding her through the process could get it done quicker, and help both her and Shiftertown.

"I can't tell you until you win the contract." Eric said. He met her gaze, not disguising anything in his. "Please."

End of Chapter One

Pride Mates

Shifters Unbound
Book One
by Jennifer Ashley

Chapter One

A girl walks into a bar …

No. A human girl walks into a Shifter bar …

The bar was empty, not yet open to customers. It looked normal—windowless walls painted black, rows of glass bottles, the smell of beer and stale air. But it wasn't normal, standing on the edge of Shiftertown like it did.

Kim told herself she had nothing to be afraid of. *They're tamed. Collared. They can't hurt you.*

"You the lawyer?" a man washing glasses asked her. He was human, not Shifter. No strange, slitted pupils, no Collar to control his aggression, no air of menace. When Kim nodded, he gestured with his cloth to a door at the end of the bar. "Knock him dead, sweetheart."

"I'll try to keep him alive." Kim pivoted and stalked away, feeling his gaze on her back.

She knocked on the door marked "Private," and a man on the other side growled, "Come."

I just need to talk to him. Then I'm done, on my way home. A trickle of moisture rolled between Kim's shoulder blades as she made herself open the door and walk inside.

A man leaned back in a chair behind a messy desk, a sheaf of papers in his hands. His booted feet were propped on the desk, his long legs a feast of blue jeans over muscle. He was a Shifter all right—thin black and silver Collar against his throat, hard, honed body, midnight-black hair, definite air of menace. When Kim entered, he stood, setting the papers aside.

Damn. He rose to a height of well over six feet and gazed at Kim with eyes blue like the morning sky. His body wasn't only honed, it was hot—big chest, wide shoulders, tight abs, firm biceps against a form-fitting black T-shirt.

"Kim Fraser?"

"That's me."

With old-fashioned courtesy, he placed a chair in front of the desk and motioned her to it. Kim felt the heat of his hand near the small of her back as she seated herself, smelled the scent of soap and male musk.

"You're Mr. Morrissey?"

The Shifter sat back down, returned his motorcycle boots to the top of the desk, and laced his hands behind his head. "Call me Liam."

The lilt in his voice was unmistakable. Kim put that with his black hair, impossibly blue eyes, and exotic name. "You're Irish."

He smiled a smile that could melt a woman at ten paces. "And who else would be running a pub?"

"But you don't own it."

Kim could have bitten out her tongue as soon as she said it. Of course he didn't own it. He was a Shifter.

His voice went frosty, the crinkles at the corners of his eyes smoothing out. "You're Brian Smith's lawyer, are you? I'm afraid I can't help you much. I don't know Brian well, and I don't know anything about what happened the night his girlfriend was murdered. It's a long time ago, now."

Disappointment bit her, but Kim had learned not to let discouragement stop her when she needed to get a job done. "Brian called you the 'go-to' guy. As in, when Shifters are in trouble, Liam Morrissey helps them out."

Liam shrugged, muscles moving the bar's logo on his T-shirt. "True. But Brian never came to me. He got into his troubles all by himself."

"I know that. I'm trying to get him *out* of trouble."

Liam's eyes narrowed, pupils flicking to slits as he retreated to the predator within him. Shifters liked to do that when assessing a situation, Brian had told her. Guess who was the prey?

Brian had done the predator-prey thing with Kim at first. He'd stopped when he began to trust her, but Kim didn't think she'd ever get used to it. Brian was her first Shifter client, the first Shifter, in fact, she'd ever seen outside a television news story. Twenty years Shifters had been acknowledged to exist, but Kim had never met one.

It was well known that they lived in their enclave on the east side of Austin, near the old airport, but she'd never come over to check them out. Some human women did, strolling the streets just outside Shiftertown, hoping for glimpses—and more—of the Shifter men who were reputed to be strong, gorgeous, and well endowed. Kim had once heard two women in a restaurant murmuring about their encounter with a Shifter male the night before. The phrase "Oh, my God," had been used repeatedly. Kim was as curious about them as anyone else, but she'd never summoned the courage to go near Shiftertown herself.

Then suddenly she was assigned the case of the Shifter accused of murdering his human girlfriend ten months ago. This was the first time in twenty years Shifters had caused trouble, the first time one had been put on trial. The public, outraged by the killing, wanted Shifters punished, pointed fingers at those who'd claimed the Shifters were tamed.

However, after Kim had met Brian, she'd determined that she wouldn't do a token defense. She believed his innocence, and she wanted to win. There wasn't much case law on Shifters because there'd never been any trials, at least none on record. This was to be a well-publicized trial, Kim's opportunity to make a mark, to set precedent.

Liam's eyes stayed on her, pupils still slitted. "You're a brave one, aren't you? To defend a Shifter?"

"Brave, that's me." Kim crossed her legs, pretending to relax. They picked up on your nervousness, people said. *They know when you're scared, and they use your fear.* "I don't mind telling you, this case had been a pain in the ass from the get-go."

"Humans think anything involving Shifters is a pain in the ass."

Kim shook her head. "I mean, it's been a pain in the ass because of the way it's been handled. The cops nearly had Brian signing a confession before I could get to the interrogation. At least I put a stop to that, but I couldn't get bail for him, I've been blocked by the prosecutors right and left every time I want review the evidence. Talking to you is a long shot, but I'm getting desperate. So if you don't want to see a Shifter go down for this crime, Mr. Morrissey, a little cooperation would be appreciated."

The way he pinned her with his eyes, never blinking, made her want to fold in on herself. Or run. That's what prey did—ran. And then predators chased them, cornered them.

What did this man do when he cornered his prey? He wore the Collar; he could do nothing. Right?

Kim imagined herself against a wall, his hands on either side of her, his hard body hemming her in … Heat curled down her spine.

Liam took his feet down and leaned forward, arms on the desk. "I haven't said I won't help you, lass." His gaze flicked to her blouse, whose buttons had slipped out of their top holes during her journey through Austin traffic and July heat. "Is Brian happy with you defending him? You like Shifters that much?"

Kim resisted reaching for the buttons. She could almost feel his fingers on them, undoing each one, and her heart beat faster.

"It's nothing to do with who I like. I was assigned to him, but I happen to think Brian's innocent. He shouldn't go down for something he didn't do." Kim liked her anger, because it covered up how edgy this man made her. "Besides, Brian's the only Shifter I've ever met, so I don't know whether I like them, do I?"

Liam smiled again. His eyes returned to normal, and now he looked like any other gorgeous, hard-bodied, blue-eyed Irishman. "You, love, are—"

"Feisty. Yeah, I've heard that one. Also spitfire, little go-getter, and a host of other condescending terms. But let me tell you, Mr. Morrissey, I'm a damn good lawyer. Brian's not guilty, and I'm going to save his ass."

"I was going to say *unusual*. For a human."

"Because I'm willing to believe he's innocent?"

"Because you came here, to the outskirts of Shiftertown, to see me. Alone."

The predator was back.

Why was it that when Brian looked at her like this, it didn't worry her? Brian was in jail, angry, accused of heinous crimes. A killer, according to the police. But Brian's stare didn't send shivers down her spine like Liam Morrissey's did.

"Any reason I shouldn't have come alone?" she asked, keeping her voice light. "I'm trying to prove that Shifters in general, and my client in particular, can't harm humans. I'd do a poor job of it if I was afraid to come and talk to his friends."

Liam wanted to laugh at the little—spitfire—but he kept his stare cool. She had no idea what she was walking into; Fergus, the clan leader, expected Liam to make sure it stayed that way.

Damn it all, Liam wasn't supposed to *like* her. He'd expected the usual human woman, sticks-up-their-asses, all of them, but there was something different about Kim Fraser. It wasn't just that she was small and compact, where Shifter women were tall and willowy. He liked how her dark blue eyes regarded him without fear, liked the riot of black of curls that beckoned his fingers. She'd had the sense to leave her hair alone, not force it into some unnatural shape.

On the other hand, she tried to hide her sweetly curvaceous body under a stiff gray business suit, although her body had other ideas. Her breasts wanted to burst out of the button-up blouse, and the stiletto heels only enhanced wickedly sexy legs.

No Shifter woman would dress like she did. Shifter women wore loose clothes they could quickly shed if they needed to change forms. Shorts and T-shirts were popular. So were gypsy skirts and sarongs in the summer.

Liam imagined this lady in a sarong. Her melon-firm breasts would fill out the top, and the skirt would bare her smooth thighs.

She'd be even prettier in a bikini, lolling around some rich man's pool, sipping a complicated drink. She was a lawyer—there was probably a boss in her firm who had already made her his. Or perhaps she was using said boss to climb the success ladder. Humans did that all the time. Either the bastard would break her heart, or she'd walk away happy with what she'd got out of it.

That's why we stay the hell away from humans. Brian Smith had taken up with a human woman, and look where he was now.

So why did this female raise Liam's protective instincts? Why did she make him want to move closer, inside the radius of her body heat? She wouldn't like that; humans tried to stay a few feet apart from each other unless they couldn't help it. Even lovers might do nothing more than hold hands in public.

Liam had no business thinking about passion and this woman in the same heartbeat. Fergus's instructions had been to listen to Kim, sway her, then send her home. Not that Liam was in the habit of blindly obeying Fergus.

"So why do you want to help him, love?" he asked. "You're only defending him because you drew the short straw, am I right?"

"I'm the junior in the firm, so it was handed to me, yes. But the prosecutor's office and the police have done a shitty job with this case. Rights violations all over the place. But the courts won't dismiss it, no matter how much I argue. Everyone wants a Shifter to go down, innocent or guilty."

"And why do you believe Brian didn't do it?"

"Why do you think?" Kim tapped her throat. "Because of these."

Liam resisted touching the strand of black and silver metal fused to his own neck, a small Celtic knot at the base of his throat. The Collars contained a tiny programmed chip enhanced by powerful Fae magic to keep Shifters in check, though the humans didn't want to acknowledge the magic part. The Collar shot an electric charge into a Shifter when his violent tendencies rose to the surface. If the Shifter persisted, the next dose was one of debilitating pain. A Shifter couldn't attack anyone if he was rolling around on the ground, writhing in agony.

Liam wasn't sure entirely how the Collars worked; he only knew that each became bonded to its wearer's skin and adapted to their animal form when they shifted. All Shifters living in human communities were required to wear the Collar, which were unremovable once put on. Refusing the Collar meant execution. If the Shifter tried to escape, he or she was hunted down and killed.

"You know Brian couldn't have committed a violent crime," Kim was saying. "His Collar would have stopped him."

"Let me guess. Your police claim the Collar malfunctioned?"

"Yep. When I suggest having it tested, I'm greeted with all kinds of reasons it can't be. The Collar can't be removed, and anyway it would be too dangerous to have Brian Collarless if he could be. Also too dangerous to provoke him to violence and see if the Collar stops him. Brian's been calm since he was brought in. Like he's given up." She looked glum. "I hate to see someone give up like that."

"You like the underdog?"

She grinned at him with red lips. "You could say that, Mr. Morrissey. Me and the underdog go back a long way."

Liam liked her mouth. He liked imagining it on his body, on certain parts of his anatomy in particular. He had no business thinking that, but the thoughts triggered a physical reaction below the belt.

Weird. He'd never even considered having sex with a human before. He didn't find human women attractive; Liam preferred to be in his big cat form for sex. He found sex that way much more satisfying. With Kim, he'd have to remain human.

His gaze strayed to her unbuttoned collar. Of course, it might not be so bad to be human with her ...

What the hell am I thinking? Liam's instructions had been clear, and Liam agreeing to them had been the only way Fergus had allowed Kim to come to Shiftertown at all. Fergus wasn't keen on a human woman having charge of Brian's case, not that they had any choice. Fergus had been pissed about Brian's arrest from the beginning and thought the Shifters should back off and stay out of it. Almost like he believed Brian was guilty.

But Fergus lived down on the other side of San Antonio, and what he didn't know wouldn't hurt him. Liam's father trusted Liam to handle this his own way, and Liam would.

"So what do you expect from me, love?" he asked Kim. "Want to test *my* Collar?"

"No, I want to know more about Brian, about Shifters and the Shifter community. Who Brian's people are, how he grew up, what it's like to live in a Shifter enclave." She smiled again. "Finding six independent witnesses who swear he was nowhere near the victim at the time in question wouldn't hurt either."

"Oh, is that all? Bloody miracles is what you want, darling."

She wrapped a dark curl around her finger. "Brian said that you're the Shifter people talk to most. Shifters and humans alike."

It was true that Shifters came to Liam with their troubles. His father, Dylan Morrissey, was master of this Shiftertown, second in power in the whole clan.

Humans knew little about the careful hierarchy of the Shifter clans and prides—packs for Lupines—and still less about how informally but efficiently everything got done. Dylan was the Morrissey pride leader and the leader of this Shiftertown, and Fergus was the clan leader for the Felines of South Texas, but Shifters with a problem sought out Liam or his brother Sean for a chat. They'd meet in the bar or at the coffee shop around the corner. *So, Liam, can you ask your father to look into it for me?*

No one would petition Dylan or Fergus directly. That wasn't done. But chatting about things to Liam over coffee, that was fine and didn't draw attention to the fact that the person in question had troubles.

Everyone would know anyway, of course. Life in a Shiftertown reminded Liam very much of life in the Irish village he'd lived near until they'd come to Texas twenty years ago. Everyone knew everything about everyone, and news traveled, lightning-swift, from one side of the village to the other.

"Brian never came to me," he said. "I never knew anything about this human girl until suddenly the police swoop in here and arrest him. His mother struggled out of bed to watch her son be dragged away. She didn't even know why for days."

Kim watched Liam's blue eyes harden. The Shifters were angry about Brian's arrest, that was certain. Citizens of Austin had tensely waited for the

Shifters to make trouble after the arrest, to break free and try to retaliate with violence, but Shiftertown remained quiet. Kim wondered why, but she wasn't about to ask right now and risk angering the one person who might help her.

"Exactly my point," she said. "This case has been handled badly from start to finish. If you help me, I can spring Brian and make a point at the same time. You don't mess with people's rights, not even Shifters'."

Liam's eyes grew harder, if that were possible. It was like looking at living sapphire. "I don't give a damn about making a point. I give a damn about Brian's family."

All right, so she'd miscalculated about what would motivate him. "In that case, Brian's family will be happier with him outside prison, not inside."

"He won't go to prison, love. He'll be executed, and you know it. No waiting twenty years on death row, either. They'll kill him, and they'll kill him fast."

That was true. The prosecutor, the county sheriff, the attorney general, and even the governor, wanted an example made of Brian. There hadn't been a Shifter attack in twenty years, and the Texas government wanted to assure the world that they weren't going to allow one now.

"So are you going to help me save him?" Kim asked. If he wanted to be direct and to the point, fine. So could she. "Or let him die?"

Anger flickered through Liam's eyes again, then sorrow and frustration. Shifters were emotional people from what she'd seen in Brian, not bothering to hide what they felt. Brian had lashed out at Kim many times before he'd grudgingly acknowledged that she was on his side.

If Liam decided to stonewall her, Brian had said, Kim had no hope of getting cooperation from the other Shifters. Even Brian's own mother would take her cue from Liam.

Liam had the look of a man who didn't take shit from anyone. A man used to giving the orders himself, but so far he hadn't seemed brutal. He could make his voice go soft and lilting, reassuring, friendly. He was a defender, she guessed. A protector of his people.

Was he deciding whether to protect Brian? Or whether to turn his back?

Liam's gaze flicked past her to the door, every line of his body coming alert. Kim's nerves made her jump. "What is it?"

Liam got out of his chair and started around the desk at the same time the door scraped open and another man—another Shifter—walked in.

Liam's expression changed. "Sean." He clasped the other Shifter's arms and pulled him into a hug.

More than a hug. Kim watched, open-mouthed, as Liam wrapped his arms around the other man, gathered him close, and nuzzled his cheek.

End of Chapter One

Read on for the
Short story

Shifter Made
Shifters Unbound
Prequel

(How the
Sword of the Guardian
came to be)

Shifter Made

Shifters Unbound
Prequel
(Short Story)
by Jennifer Ashley

Chapter One

Baile Ícín, near Dingle, Ciarrai, 1400

"Smith."

Niall knew without looking up from his anvil that the woman who addressed him was Fae—Sidhe, the villagers called them. He could smell her, a bright, sticky-sweet stench that humans found irresistible.

He kept his head bent over his task. Mending a cooking crane for a village woman was far more important than speaking to a Fae. Besides, his name wasn't Smith, and if she couldn't call Niall by his real name he saw no need to answer.

"Shifter, I command you," she said.

Niall continued hammering. Wind poured through the open doors, carrying the scent of brine, fish, and clean air, which still could not cover the stench of Fae.

"Shifter."

"This forge is filled with iron, lass," Niall said. "And Shifters don't obey Fae anymore. Did you not hear that news a hundred and fifty years ago?"

"I have a spell that keeps my sensitivity to iron at bay. For a time. Long enough to deal with you."

She had a voice like clearest water, and Niall finally looked up, curiosity winning over animosity. A tall woman in flowing silk stood on his threshold, her body haloed by the setting sun. Her pale hair hung to her knees in a score of thin braids, and she had the dark eyes and slender, pointed ears common to her kind. She was beautiful in an ethereal sort of way. But then all Fae were beautiful, the evil bastards.

The wind boiling up over the sea cliffs cut through the doorway, and the woman shivered. Niall raised his brows. He'd never caught a Fae doing a thing so normal as shiver.

He thrust the end of the crane into the fire, sending sparks into the darkness. "Come in out of the weather, girl. You'll be freezing in those flimsy clothes."

"My name is Alanna, and I'm hardly a girl."

She had to be young if she responded to Niall's condescension, or at least naïve. Fae lived so long and never changed much once they were fully grown that it was difficult to tell what age they were. She could be twenty-five or four hundred and fifty.

Alanna stepped all the way into the forge, darting nervous glances at the iron—the anvil, his tools, the piece of crane he was mending. "I've been sent to give you a commission."

"You were sent, were you? Poor lass. You must have offended someone high up to be handed the thankless task of entering the mortal world to speak to a Shifter."

Her cheeks colored but her tone remained haughty. "I've come to ask you to forge a sword. I believe you were once a sword maker of some repute."

"In days gone by. Now I'm a humble blacksmith, making practical things for villagers here and on the Great Island."

"Nonetheless, I am certain you retained your skill. The sword is to have a blade three feet in length, made of silver. The hilt to be of bronze."

Niall drew the crane from the fire, set it on his anvil, and quickly hammered the glowing end into shape. "No," he said.

"What?"

He enunciated each word. "No, I will not make such a damn fool weapon for a Fae. For anyone."

Alanna regarded him, slack-jawed, a very un-Fae like expression. Fae were cold beings, barely bringing themselves to speak civilly to anything non-Fae. Fae had once bred Shifters to hunt and fight for them, and they regarded Shifters as animals, one step below humans.

This woman looked troubled, confused, even embarrassed. "You will do this."

"I will not."

"You must."

Was that panic now? Niall thrust the iron crane back into the fire and straightened up.

The Fae woman stepped back, and Niall fought a smile. Niall was big, even for a Shifter. His arms were strong from a lifetime of smithy work, and he'd always been tall. Alanna would come up to his chin if he stood next to her; her slender hands would get lost in his big ones. He could break her like a twig if he chose, and by the fear in her black eyes, she thought he'd choose to.

"Listen to me, lass. Go back to wherever you came from, and tell them that Shifters take orders no more. We are no longer your slaves, or your hunters, or your pets. We are finished." He turned back to pump the bellows, sweat trickling down his bare back. "Besides, silver won't make a decent sword. The metal's too soft."

"Spells have been woven through the metal to make it as strong as steel. You will work it the same as you would any other sword."

"I will, will I? Fae don't like swords in any case—your preferred weapon is the bow. Not to mention the copper knife for gouging out other beings' hearts, usually while the heart is still beating."

"That is only the priests, and only when we need to make a sacrifice."

"Sacrifice, you call it? Seems like it's not much of a sacrifice for you but hard on the one who's losing his heart."

"That's really none of your affair. You need to make the sword for me. What we use it for doesn't concern you."

"You are wrong about that." Niall lifted the crane again, quickly hammered it into its final shape, and thrust it into his cooling barrel. Water and metal met with a hiss, and steam boiled into the air. "Anything I make has a little part of meself in it. I'm not putting that into a sacrificial weapon you'll stick it into helpless animals or humans or Shifters who never did any harm to you."

Her brow clouded. "A piece of yourself? Blood or a bit of skin …?"

"Not literally, you ignorant woman. I don't christen it with blood, like some Fae priest. I mean I put a bit of my soul in everything I craft. Gods know I wouldn't want Fae touching anything that's come close to my soul."

Her face flamed, and her look was now … ashamed? "Shifter, I must take this sword back with me at first light."

Last light was now streaming through the door, the spring air turning even more frigid. "And where would I be getting time to craft such a thing before morning? Sword-working is a long business, and I have sons to look after. Go on home and tell them you couldn't bully the big, mean Shifter."

"Damn you." Alanna clenched her fists, eyes sparkling. "Are all Shifters this bloody stubborn? I thought I could do this without hurting you."

Niall looked her up and down. Fae could work powerful magic, without doubt, but not much in the human world. They'd given up that power to retreat to the safety of their own realm, while Shifters had learned to adapt and remain in the world of humans. Fae still had magic out here—minor spells, glamour, and misdirection, not that they didn't use those to lure human beings to their deaths.

"Could you hurt me, lass? In this forge full of iron? I lost my mate ten years ago. That hurt me more than anything in the world ever could. I doubt you could match that pain, no matter how many spells you can throw at me."

"No?" Alanna asked, her voice ringing. "What about if you lost your cubs?"

Niall was across the room and had her pinned against the wall before the echo of her words died, the iron bar he'd just cooled in the water pressed across the her pale throat.

Chapter Two

The Shifter was stronger than she'd imagined, and the iron against Alanna's skin burned. The spell that her brother had grudgingly let his chief magician chant over her kept the worst at bay, but the bar felt white hot.

Odors of sweat, fire, smoke, and metal poured off the Shifter called Niall. He'd scraped his black hair into a tight braid, the style emphasizing his high cheekbones and sharp nose, the touch of Fae ancestry that had never disappeared from Shifters. His hard jaw was studded with dark whiskers, wet with sweat from his labors. The whiskers and sweat made him seem so raw, so animal-like. Fae men were beardless, their skin paper smooth, and she'd never seen one do anything so gauche as sweat.

Studying the Shifter's stubbled chin kept Alanna from having to look into his eyes. Those eyes had been deep green when she'd entered the forge; now they were nearly white, his pupils slitted like a cat's. He *was* a cat, a predatory cat bred from several species of ancient wildcats, and any second now he'd tear her apart.

And then his two sons would die.

Niall's towering rage held her as firmly as the iron bar. "You touch my cubs, bitch, and you'll be learning what pain truly is."

"If you do as I say, they won't be hurt at all."

"You'll not go near them."

"It's too late for that. They've already been taken. Make the sword, and you'll get them back."

The Shifter roared. His face elongated, and animal lips pulled back from fangs. He didn't shift all the way, but the hand that held the bar sprouted finger-long claws.

At the moment Alanna hated all Shifters and all Fae, especially her brother Kieran, who'd told her that subduing the Shifter would be simple. *They will do anything to protect their whelps. We carry them off, and he'll whimper at your feet.*

Niall O'Connell, master sword maker of the old Kingdom of Ciarrai, wasn't whimpering, or anywhere near her feet. His fury could tear down the forge and crumble the cliff face into the sea.

"Make the sword." Now Alanna was the one pleading. "Craft the sword, and the little ones go free."

Niall's face shifted back into his human one, but his eyes remained white. "Where are they?"

"They will be released when you complete the sword."

Niall shoved her into the wall. "Damn you, woman, *where are they*?"

"In the realm of Faerie."

The Shifter's pupils returned to human shape, his eye color darkening to jade as grief filled them. Niall's shoulders slumped, but the iron never moved from Alanna's throat. "Gone, then," he whispered.

"No," Alanna said quickly. "If you give me the sword, they will be set free. He assured me they would not be harmed."

"Who did? Who is this Fae bastard who's taken my children?"

"My brother. Kieran."

"Kieran ..."

"Prince Kieran of Donegal."

"There was a Kieran of Donegal in Shifter stories of long ago. A vicious bastard that a pack of Lupines finally hunted and killed. Only decent thing the bloody dogs have ever done."

"My brother is his grandson."

"Which makes you his granddaughter." Niall peered at her. "You don't seem all that pleased to be running this errand for your royal brother. Why did he send you?"

"None of your affair." Enemies saw your compassion as weakness and used that against you, Kieran had told her. Kieran certainly used every advantage over his enemies—and his friends as well.

"Back to that, are you, lass? What assurance do I have that you'll not simply kill my cubs whether I make the sword for you or not?"

Alanna shifted the tiniest bit, trying to ease the pain of the bar on her throat. "You have my pledge."

"And what worth is that to me?"

"My pledge that if your children are harmed, you may take my life. I wasn't just sent as the messenger, Shifter. I was sent to be your hostage."

*** *** ***

Even through his pain, his grief, and his gut-wrenching fear, Niall couldn't deny that the Fae woman had courage. He could kill her right now, and she knew it. She offered her life in exchange for his sons with a steady voice, even though she obviously knew that a Shifter whose cubs were threatened was more dangerous than an erupting volcano. And even though she'd said she'd been given a protective spell against iron, Niall knew the cold bar hurt her.

Slowly he lifted it from her throat. Alanna rubbed her neck, though the bar had left no mark.

Niall stopped himself having any sympathy. She and her brother had taken his boys, Marcus and Piers, who were ten and twelve as humans counted years.

He looked past her to the darkening night, to the mists gathering on the cliff path, to the Great Island silhouetted by the blood-red sky. "My youngest, Marcus, he likes to fish," he said. "The human way with a pole and hook. Will he be able to fish where he is?"

Alanna shook her head. "The game and the fish in the rivers are for Kieran only."

"My mate died of bringing him in, poor love. She was a beautiful woman, was Caitlin, so tall and strong." Niall looked Alanna up and down. "Nothing like you."

"No, I don't suppose she was."

Shifter women tended to be as tall as the males. They were fast runners, wild in bed, and laughed a lot. Caitlin had laughed all the time.

"Piers, now. He likes to craft things. He'll be a smith like me. He likes to watch the iron get red hot and bend into whatever shape he tells it. He'd love to have watched me make this sword."

Alanna said nothing, only looked at him.

Niall knew why he was saying these things. He was letting himself start to grieve.

Deep in his heart, he didn't believe Prince Kieran would agree to release his sons. Fae didn't play fair. Niall might be allowed to take Alanna's life in vengeance for his sons' death, but it would be an empty vengeance. He would have no one left. No mate, no cubs, no one left in his pride.

Niall lived here on the edge of this human village called Baile Icin, because the other members of his pride and clan had died out. Shifters took mates from other clans, but there weren't as many females as males anymore, and other clans were few and far between. The Shifter race was diminishing.

"You'll make the sword then?" Alanna asked, breaking his thoughts.

She didn't have to sound so eager. "I don't have much bloody choice, do I?"

Her eyes softened. "I am sorry."

Sympathy, from a Fae? Had the world gone mad today?

"You will be, lass. If my cubs are hurt in any way, you'll be the first to be very, very sorry. Your brother, now, he'll be even sorrier still. So show me this silver and let's be getting on with it."

Chapter Three

Forging a sword was a different thing entirely from the usual practical ironworks Niall produced for the humans of the village. Niall never asked Alanna why he'd been chosen for this task, because he already knew.

Once upon a time, Niall O'Connell had been a master sword maker, before Ciarrai had been made an Earldom by the bloody English. He'd created beautiful weapons used for deadly purpose in the last Fae-Shifter war. The Shifters had won that war, though Niall knew much of their victory had been due to luck—the Fae had already been losing power in the mortal world, and the Shifters had only made their retreat into the Faerie realms inevitable.

It wasn't often that Shifters from different clans and species worked together, but at that point, Lupine, Feline, and Bear had fought side by side. The

Fae had conceded defeat and vanished into their realm behind the mists.

Well, *conceded defeat* was too strong a phrase. The Fae had gone, killing, burning, and pillaging behind them. Fae didn't care whether their victims were children, breeding mothers, or humans who just happened to be in the wrong place at the wrong time.

Niall still had his sword-making tools kept safely in a chest at the back of the forge. He hadn't touched them in years. He shook his head to himself as he laid out his tongs and hammer, grinding stone and chisel. This sword wouldn't be good, strong steel, but soft silver, which was daft, even if she claimed it was spelled to work like steel. He could craft such a thing, but it would only be good as a trinket.

He briefly considered mixing a bit of iron into the hilt to debilitate any Fae who touched it, but he knew such a trick would make his sons' deaths even more certain. Not that he believed the Fae prince would let Niall live either, in any case. But Niall would take out the Fae bitch when they came for him. Prince Kieran would watch his sister die before he killed Niall.

Niall glanced at Alanna as he pounded out the bar of metal she'd brought him. She'd found a stool and seated herself on it near the fire. She did look cold, the silly woman, probably not used to the harsh clime of the Irish west coast. The Faerie realms, he'd heard, were misty and soft all the time, which was why she wore flimsy silk robes and let her braids flow. Fae women didn't have to bundle their hair out of the wind.

After a few quick looks at her, he realized that Alanna wasn't staring sightlessly at the forge, or watching him beat the blade. She was studying *him*.

Her gaze roved his bare back and the muscles of his arms, as though she'd never seen a half-clothed man before. She probably hadn't. Fae were cold people, not liking to be touched, preferring robes, jewels, and other fussy things to bare skin. They rarely did anything as crude as coupling, bodily seduction being almost as distasteful to them as iron. Shifters, on the other hand, loved breeding and loved children, children being all that more precious because so few survived.

"Are you a virgin, then, lass?" Niall asked her.

Alanna jumped. "What?"

"A virgin. If it doesn't hurt your pristine ears for me to ask it. Are you?"

"No."

Interesting. Fae women didn't lie with males unless they absolutely had to. "You have a lover then? A husband?"

"No." The word was more angry now. "It is none of your affair."

"You like to say that, I notice. Did you have a babe?"

"A child? No." Again, the chill anger.

"I'm sorry, love."

"Why?"

"That must have hurt you."

When a Shifter woman was childless it was an impossible sorrow to her. As dangerous as breeding was for Shifters, females were happy to risk it to bring in cubs. "I imagine 'tis different for a Fae woman." The Fae were so long-lived they didn't bear many children. Fae women who did like children often stole them from humans, rather than bearing their own, raising them to be their doting little slaves.

"It did hurt me," she said.

Niall saw the pain in her eyes. She looked so out of place, sitting in his forge, her strange, elegant robes already soiled from the dust and soot. He never thought he'd feel sorry for a Fae, but the sadness on her face was real.

"Did your lover not want a child?" Niall asked gently.

"My lover, as you call him, died." Alanna's jaw was fixed, rigid. "We tried to have a child, but I don't know whether it was even possible."

"Fae do breed. I've seen your wee ones." Even crueler than the adults, unfortunately.

"My lover was human."

Surprise stilled Niall's hands. "A human man? Let me guess. A slave?" He couldn't keep the disgust out of his voice.

"He had been captured, yes." She met his look defiantly. "But not by me."

"Oh, that makes it all right then. Whose slave was he? You're royal brother's?"

"Yes. It was a long time ago."

One of her brother's slaves, made into her lover. A typical story of Fae cruelty except for the grief in her eyes. He wasn't imagining that.

He bent over his task again. "How long ago?" he asked.

"One hundred years."

"And you loved this man? Or pretended to?"

Her silence was so flint-hard that Niall raised his head again. She was glaring at him. "Did you love your mate?" she asked in a sharp voice.

"I won't apologize for my question. You are the one coercing me into helping the bastard who stole my children. I'll answer yours—yes, I loved her more than my own life."

"My answer is the same."

She met his gaze without flinching. The pain in her dark eyes wasn't false and neither was the loneliness, and Alanna didn't look ashamed of either.

Niall went back to pounding. After a time he asked, "So what happened to this human male so worthy of the love of a Fae woman?"

"My brother killed him."

Niall stopped. "The very brother who sent you here? Why?"

"Because Dubhan dared to touch me."

"The man was your slave. He wouldn't have had a choice."

Alanna's face grew cold again. "You see everything through Shifter eyes. Dubhan was my brother's slave, so of course you believe I forced him to service me. I told you, I loved him. I freed him, I fled with him to the human world, and we became lovers. Until my brother found us."

"You sneaked out of the Faerie realms to become lover to a human?" Niall's astonishment, and respect for her, rose. "You are an amazing and brave lass."

"I was foolish, as it turned out. I should have sent him off and not tried to stay with him. Kieran would have forgotten about one slave in time, but he never forgave me for letting a lesser being touch me."

"Which is why he sent you here to become hostage to a Shifter."

"I am my brother's prisoner and in disgrace. I am forced to do his bidding."

"Does he not fear that while you're in the human world you'll break away and flee him?"

Alanna shrugged. "I have nowhere to go, and unlike Shifters, I cannot pass for a human. The spell that lets me resist iron will wear off." She shivered. "And it is so cold here."

Niall rose, fetched the woolen cloak he'd thrown aside when he'd started to work, and draped it over her shoulders. She looked up in surprise, jerking her hand away when his brushed hers.

He'd thought her overly slender when she first walked in, but now he saw that this was a trick of the loose-flowing garments. Her bosom was round and full, her waist nipped in above strong hips. Her face was delicate, a little too pointed for Niall's taste, but her dark eyes drew him in. Her braids outlined her pointed ears, but the ears didn't look as strange and unnatural close up. She was flesh, not cold marble, her skin flushing as she warmed from the fire and the cloak.

"You could pass for human," Niall said as he went back to the forge.

"Unlikely. Look at me."

"I just did." Niall took up the heated bar with his tongs and tapped the rapidly cooling metal. "If you wore your hair loose to hide your ears and dressed in human clothes instead of fancy frippery, no one would look twice." He considered this as he flipped the bar. "No, they'd look twice, because you're a beautiful woman, but unless you shouted it, I don't believe they'd realize you were Fae. Most humans don't believe in the Fae any longer, anyway. They pretend to—they avoid the stone circles at night and put out milk to appease the sprites, but deep down, they believe only in hard work, exhaustion, and God. Bless them."

"You care for them," Alanna said, sounding surprised. "But you're Shifter."

"If you lived in the human world before, you might have noticed that Shifters are not all that thick on the ground. We might be stronger and more cunning than humans, we might be able to change into ferocious beasts when we wish to, but we need humans in order to survive."

"Do the humans in this village know you're Shifter?"

Niall shrugged. "They know I'm different, but as I said, they don't much believe in the *other* anymore. But they know I'm a good smith and that the villages round about get left in peace now that I live here."

"You're good to them."

"It's survival, love. We each have what the other needs. 'Tis the only way Shifters are going to last."

"The Fae chose to retreat." Alanna said it almost to herself, as though she didn't expect an answer. "We sought the mists of Faerie."

"Aye, that you did."

She fell silent, but Alanna was difficult to ignore as he continued work, and not just because of the distinct Fae smell, which didn't seem so terrible now. Perhaps he was growing used to it.

Niall sensed her presence like a bright light—her beauty, her sorrow, her courage in coming here when she knew she'd likely lose her life. Fae princes could be mean bastards, and the fact that she'd defied this Kieran about the human slave spoke much of her.

Once Niall had the metal thin enough, he heated it again, ready to shape it. As he set the blade on the anvil and took up his hammer, he felt her breath on his shoulder.

"Wait."

"Metal's hot, lass. It won't wait."

"I need to layer in some spells."

His eyes narrowed. "What is this sword for? For ceremony, I know, not fighting, but what sort of ceremony, exactly?"

"I'm not certain myself."

Niall's grip tightened on his hammer. "Don't lie to me now. If you're putting in the spells, you know what they do."

"I cannot tell you. Please, if you know, then your sons will die."

"I think they'll die anyway, and I think you know that too. Tell me this much—is the sword meant to hurt Shifters?"

Alanna said nothing, but the look in her eyes spoke volumes. He read guilt there, anguish, grief, anger.

Niall shoved the bar from the anvil with a clatter. He sat down on the floor, his hammer falling to his side. "You're asking me to save my sons by forging a weapon against Shifters? What kind of monster are you?"

Alanna sank to her knees beside him, her silks whispering across his skin. "Niall of Baile Icin, I ask you to please trust me. Make the sword. All will be well."

Niall growled. "Your bastard brother will slaughter my boys the minute he gets this piece of metal in his hands. He knows I'll kill you in retaliation, and then he'll kill me, and laugh about it. That is how things will play out."

Alanna shook her head, her braids touching his bare shoulders. "Not if you trust me. I cannot tell you everything, but you must make the sword the way I have instructed." She put her hand on his shoulder—Fae, who didn't like to touch. "Please, Niall."

"And why should I trust you? Because you once bedded a human? Should I believe you have compassion for the whole world then?"

"Because of a vow I once made. I will never let your children come to harm. I promise."

Fae had a way of enchanting, of charming. Niall knew that, had experienced it firsthand. But Alanna's pleading look was different somehow from the Fae who'd once spelled Shifters to be slaves to them. Fae charmed by being too brightly beautiful, too desirable, stirring a person into a frenzy before they knew what happened. Alanna didn't make Niall feel frenzied or dazzled. He was angry and sick, tired and sad.

When Shifters lost loved ones, they retreated from the rest of the pride or pack to be alone with their grief. A survival instinct, he supposed, because in that gut-ripping sorrow, they had no desire to fight or hunt or even eat. A wildcat or wolf or bear might weaken the pack by refusing to fight, and so the Shifter took himself away until the worst passed. Or he died.

Alanna's hand on Niall's shoulder was cool, cutting through his instinct to seek solace. Her fingers were soothing to his roasting skin, and her fragrance no longer seemed cloying, but fresh like mint.

"Please," she said.

Niall got to his feet and pulled her up with him. "You ask much of me."

"I know."

Alanna's eyes weren't black, as he'd thought, but deep brown with black flecks, her wide pupils making them seem darker. Her hair was like fine threads of white gold, metal so delicate that the merest touch could break it.

Niall stepped away from her, fetched the half-formed blade, and thrust it back into the fire. "And you wager your life on me trusting you?"

"Yes," she said. "Will you?"

Niall looked down at her, his insides knotting. "Looks as though I'll have to, doesn't it?"

She gave him a smile of pure relief. "Thank you, Niall."

Niall turned back to work, wishing her smile didn't warm him so.

Chapter Four

Alanna let her hand hover over the red-hot blade Niall laid on the anvil, the metal's heat touching her skin. She murmured the spell, watching the curled Fae runes sear into the metal and disappear.

Niall did not trust her, and she couldn't force him to, but she was relieved he'd at least let her do the spells. Alanna couldn't ask more of him, not without fear that Kieran would discover what she was doing.

Niall beat the sword after the runes faded, as she instructed, then put it back into the fire. Again and again they repeated the pattern—Niall hammering the blade, Alanna chanting her spells.

They worked side-by-side, shoulders brushing, both sweating from the fire, both breathing hard from exertion. Spell casting, especially spells as powerful and far-reaching as these, took stamina.

Alanna soon set aside the cloak and pushed up her long sleeves.

The stench of sweating Shifter didn't seem as bad now. Niall had, well, an *honest* smell, one that came of hard work and caring. He protected the people of this village the same way he protected his children, a fact that Alanna wouldn't relate to Kieran. If her brother thought the villagers important to Niall, Kieran would find some way to use that against him.

When Niall said the sword needed to rest, he shoved it into a barrel of ash, wiped the sweat from his face, and led her from the forge. The dirt track outside hugged the cliffs above the sea, Niall's shop being at the very end of the high street—if the muddy track between the houses could be termed a high street. The western ocean pounded away below them, the moon glowing on the black bulk of the nearby island.

At first Alanna worried that Niall had brought her to the cliffs for some nefarious purpose—perhaps tossing her over and ridding himself of a troubling Fae—but he simply stood looking out over the dark ocean, breathing in the bracing air.

"You know we'll never finish on time," he said. "Blades have to be heated and rested a number of times to make the metal strong, and then I still have to grind the blade and make the hilt."

"You'll finish."

"You sound certain."

"The spells I'm using will temper the blade faster than your process by hand," she said. "When we go back, you'll be ready to grind it."

"I'm not ready to go back yet, lass."

He had to be freezing out here without a shirt, the icy wind from the sea whipping his short braid. His eyes were green even in the faint moonlight, hard green, not Shifter white-green.

Alanna didn't flinch when he cupped her neck with his big, rough hand. The touch of others had always sickened her, until she'd met Dubhan. She wondered what sort of strange Fae woman she was that she'd fallen in love with a human man and now didn't mind that a Shifter pulled her into his embrace.

Niall's face was lined with dirt and soot, but by now hers couldn't be much better. His hard body cut the wind, and she melded into him as he scooped her against him and kissed her.

His kiss was harder even than Dubhan's, firm mouth opening hers, his whiskers burning her lips. He tasted raw, of this wild land of Eire, of a bite of ale, and of himself.

Niall eased back, and Alanna shivered, not willing to let go of his warmth. The wind cut through her, but she scarcely noticed it.

"This might be our last night, you and I," he said. "The last night of our lives."

"Yes."

Niall kissed her lips, her cheeks, her neck. "Maybe 'tis Fae enchantment that you're pouring over me, but I suddenly want you with me in my bed for this last night."

She nodded, breathless. "Yes."

"You agree that it's our last night? Or are you saying you'll share my bed?"

"Both."

He cupped her face in his hands. "Be certain, Alanna."

"I am. Very certain."

Niall took her hand. The night gusted cold, but Alanna felt very warm with her hand swallowed by his. She knew she was foolish for going with him, but she no longer cared. If this didn't work she, Niall, and his children would die. She and Niall could find comfort in each other for one last night.

Niall led her behind the forge and to a neat cottage with a garden in front. She saw signs of his family—small boots, scattered tools, half-whittled pieces of wood—animals the boys had been carving when they'd been snatched by Kieran's men.

Niall avoided looking at the carvings as he led Alanna inside and up to the loft, where neat pallets had been made up for the night. Niall stripped without a word, revealing a body of solid muscle, male beauty sculpted by nature and the ancient Fae. Shifters had been bred to be superior in strength, speed, and stamina, and they'd also been made to be beautiful.

He put his hands on his hips, unashamed that his wanting was plain to see. "Are you not getting undressed?"

Alanna untied the complicated tapes that held her gown to her body and let it fall in one piece. She liked the appreciative way Niall looked at her nakedness instead of with the loathing or indifference she'd have expected of a Shifter. His gaze lingered on her breasts, his eyes dark and soft.

Alanna went to him. He raked his hands through her braids and tilted her head back to kiss her deeply. His hardness pressed her belly, his arousal long and thick. She'd always heard that Shifters were more endowed than humans or even Fae, and she decided that this rumor was true.

Niall's huge, work-worn hand cupped her breast, thumb brushing the tip. He kissed her neck, nipping her a little before he kissed her mouth again.

Alanna had loved Dubhan, and she always would. The fact that loving him had caused his death had haunted her for a century. But this Shifter would never go easily to her brother's men, never would give up without a fight. Niall could have killed her outright when she'd announced that Kieran had kidnapped his cubs, but he was giving her the gift of his trust—well, perhaps not his full trust, but at least his hope.

Niall lifted her and set her gently on the pallet. He came down with her, stretching his warm body on top of hers.

"You're such a bit of a thing." He closed his hand around her wrist. "See? So fragile."

"I'm stronger than you know."

"I know, lass. You have Fae strength, but I've never seen it packaged in such beauty."

Was he trying to melt her heart? The big, strong Shifter with loneliness and sorrow in his eyes? She suddenly wanted to hold him and heal all his hurts.

Niall had something else on his mind besides healing just now. He parted her thighs with a soothing hand and slid himself inside her.

Alanna's eyes widened as he filled her, so big, but feeling so *good*. What a wonder that a huge, barbaric, beast of a Shifter could be so gentle.

He stayed gentle as he began the rhythm of lovemaking, his head bowed, his braid sliding across his shoulder. Alanna cupped his hips, urging him with hands and mouth not to be *too* careful with her. Niall groaned as he sped his thrusts, kissing her as she met him stroke for stroke.

Alanna's frenzy began a few seconds before his did. They peaked together, both crying out, both holding hard, kissing and panting, hot breaths tangling. Then they wound down together, Niall kissing her face, her neck, her lips.

"You see?" Alanna whispered. "I'm perfectly fine."

"That you are, sweeting. And so am I. As you can feel inside of you."

"You mean I've not yet worn you down?"

Niall grinned and licked her upper lip. "Not by a long way, my love. Not by a long way."

He started again, this time more playfully. In spite of knowing that Niall was right, that this might be their only night together, and in spite of her worry about the choices she'd made, Alanna pulled him inside her and let herself drown in his loving.

*** *** ***

Alanna awoke an hour later to see Niall leaving the bed. She lay in the warm nest they'd made, enjoying the view of his buttocks as he bent to fetch a tunic. Their gazes met when Niall straightened up to slide it on.

His eyes changed to the feral cat within him before returning to deep green. "You're such a beautiful lass." He leaned down to kiss her, his lips warm.

She savored the kiss. "Where are you going?"

"The sword won't get finished by itself. It's not going to be a very good weapon made so hasty."

"My spells will hold it together." The point was for Shifter craftsmanship and Fae magic to join.

Niall descended to the lower floor, and she heard him poke up a fire and clatter crockery. She pulled on her robes and followed him downstairs to find him setting out ale and bread and a hard chunk of cheese.

"I'll do that," she said as he started to slice the bread. "You go to the forge, and I'll bring the breakfast." Niall raised his brows, and she smiled. "I used to make Dubhan breakfast. He was surprised I could do it."

Niall shrugged, set down the knife, and kissed her cheek. She turned her head to meet his kiss, determined to enjoy this very brief time they had together. Her hand closed around the knife handle, and she gasped.

"Damn," she said. Alanna looked at her fingers, which were creased with light burns. "The spell is wearing off." She sucked on her fingertips.

Niall picked up the knife and quickly cut slices of bread and cheese. "What did you do when you lived in the human world before?"

She took her fingers out of her mouth. "Dubhan found copper and bronze knives for me."

"You need to go back to Faerie."

"When the sword is finished."

They assessed each other again, like enemies who'd learned to respect each others' skills. Niall brushed her hair back from her face and kissed her forehead.

"Eat your breakfast, love, and we'll finish the sword. Whatever comes, we'll make the best damn sword that ever was."

Alanna didn't reach for the plate. "Let us finish now. I don't need sustenance the same way Shifters and humans do."

"Eat the food, woman. You're weak here, and with all this iron about, you'll be getting weaker."

"Yes, dear." Alanna sat down, slanting him a demure glance. "Whatever you say, dear."

His eyes narrowed. "Your brother doesn't know what a feisty witch he's harboring, does he?"

She sent him a grin. "'Tis best that way, do you not think?"

"Vixen." Niall leaned down and kissed her. "To think, when you walked into my forge, I thought you cold and brittle."

"You warmed me, Niall."

"Aye, I wrapped that cloak around you."

"That is not what I meant."

Niall gave her another seductive kiss. "I know."

He grabbed bread and cheese, took a gulp of ale, and banged out of the cottage, sending chill air sweeping through the room. Alanna shivered again, but without the loathing she'd had last night. It was cold in this human place called Baile Icin, but with Niall to keep her warm, she thought she could weather it.

Chapter Five

Whatever else Alanna's magics did, they certainly sped up the forging process. Alanna chanted more spells, and Niall watched runes appear and disappear as he formed the tang, made the hilt, and ground the blade. Alanna closed her eyes for the last spell, sweat standing out on her brow as her musical voice pronounced the words.

The last set of fiery runes faded to be replaced by fine lines that etched themselves all over the sword and hilt. Those lines didn't fade but joined in continuous, interlinked patterns, interwoven with runes, as though they bound the sword and hilt together. Even though Alanna ceased speaking, Niall thought he still heard her voice, soft whispers coming from the sword itself.

Niall raised the blade, finding the balance perfect, the edge sharp. If he didn't know better, he'd swear he held a sword of the best, strongest Damascus steel. He made a few sweeps, amazed at what he'd wrought.

No, what *they'd* wrought.

"We make a good sword, you and me," he said. "Now, do you mind telling me what it's for?"

Alanna hugged her chest. "Ceremonial purposes, as I said. For my brother."

"Aye. And what kind of ceremonies will he be conducting?"

"I do not want to tell you that."

Niall brought the sword around until the tip was an inch from her throat. Alanna didn't flinch, didn't move, though he saw her draw a breath. "You had better tell me now."

"If I do, you'll try to kill Kieran, and he'll destroy you, and your sons. Probably very slowly so that you will beg for their deaths. And yours. Please, do not make me watch that."

The anguish in her eyes was real, but Niall shook his head. "Sweeting, he will kill me anyway. I'd rather go out trying to take him with me."

"Niall." Alanna took one step closer, letting the tip of the sword nick her skin. A drop of Fae-blood, so dark red it was almost black, welled up from the cut and trickled across her throat. Niall quickly withdrew the sword and wiped the blood from her skin with his thumb.

"I pledged myself as hostage to you," Alanna said. "I made a promise that I would get your sons released. I will fulfill that promise. But to do it, I must again ask you to trust me. Let me take the sword to my brother, let me finish my part of the bargain. Your sons will come home to you today. *Please.*"

"You're daft, woman, do you know that? Are you planning to take this blade and stick it into your brother? Tell me you're not going to try something so stupid."

Alanna shook her head. "It's tempting, but no. He would expect me to do something like that. I imagine his bowmen would shoot me dead the moment I raised the sword."

"Good." Niall set the weapon down and pulled her close. "I'll not have you throwing yourself away on vengeance. 'Tis not worth it."

"You were ready to kill me when I first came in here."

"That was instinct. You're Fae, I'm Shifter."

"And now?"

Niall smoothed her hair, loving the satin feel of it. Even sleep-tousled and sooty, Alanna was beautiful. "Now I'm thinking you've made me feel something I've not felt in a very long time. Can a Shifter love a Fae?"

"I don't know," she said softly. "This Fae once loved a human. It might be possible for her to love a Shifter."

He cupped her cheek. "So what do we do about it?"

"Let me finish my task. Then if I am still alive, I will return to you, and we shall find out what happens between us."

Niall saw it then, her certainty she wouldn't live through whatever her brother had in mind. She knew she might have to sacrifice her life to save his children, and she was prepared to do it.

Niall drew her close. He vowed to himself, then and there, to protect her. He'd make himself trust her, whatever she was planning, because Alanna knew how to get his cubs free and he didn't. But he wouldn't let her pay with her life. Niall would protect her as a Shifter would his mate.

If they survived this, Niall would seek another clan leader and ask that leader to bless him and Alanna under the sun and the full moon, in the eyes of the God and the Goddess. Niall's own clan leader was long dead, which meant that Niall was, in fact, a clan leader—of the very small clan of himself and his sons, he thought with a grin. But he couldn't do the mating ceremony himself.

One thing at a time.

"I'm not letting you go, yet, Alanna, love," Niall said softly. He kissed her lips. "Not quiet yet."

Alanna pulled him into a deeper kiss. Niall took the sword with him as he led her to the cottage and made love to her again in the light of the rising sun.

*** *** ***

When Niall awoke in the bed later, Alanna was gone. Entirely gone—he didn't catch her scent in the cottage at all. Her silken robes were no longer hanging on the peg next to his tunic, and the sword he'd laid next to the bed had vanished.

Niall rose, naked, and shifted into his Fae-cat form.

Several thousand years before, the Fae had taken the best of every wildcat in existence and bred the Fae-cat, larger and stronger than any natural beast. Fae-cats had the strength of lions, the ferocity of tigers, the speed of cheetahs, the stealth of panthers. Each Shifter clan tended more toward one wildcat species than others, and Niall's family had always had much lion in it.

As that lion-like Fae-cat, Niall bounded down from the loft and out into dense fog that had rolled in from the sea.

Alanna wasn't in the forge. He picked up her scent on the path that led to the gently sloping mountain above the village, toward the circle of standing stones that even the most unbelieving of the villagers liked to avoid.

Mists rolled between the stones when Niall reached them, smelling all wrong. Instead of the salt and fish scent carried by the heavy fog over the village, these mists exuded an acrid smell, overlaid with the sharp scent of mint.

An entrance to Faerie. Niall regarded it with foreboding before he realized that Alanna's scent was quickly fading. His sons were in there, and now Alanna.

Without further thought, Niall leapt into the mists between two of the stones and heard something snick closed behind him.

Chapter Six

Alanna found her brother hunting, which wasn't unusual. Kieran spent most of his time hunting, or rather, having his men chase animals to him so that he could shoot them.

Kieran was every inch a Fae prince as he stood in the fog-soaked clearing. He wore a white kid tunic, soft boots, and a fur-trimmed cloak, and his white-blond hair was held back by a diamond diadem. Two men at arms flanked him, one carrying his bow; the other, his quiver of arrows.

As Alanna approached, Kieran took the bow and nocked an arrow, sighting into the woods opposite her. A few seconds later a wolf charged out of the fog, streaking for the heavy undergrowth on Alanna's side of the clearing. The wolf was larger than most, and its blue-white eyes held intelligence.

The wolf saw Alanna and veered at the last minute. Kieran's arrow, which had left the bow, bounced off a boulder where the wolf had been a second before.

Kieran shoved his bow back at his armsman and growled. "Damn you, Alanna. I've been tracking that wolf all night."

More likely his trackers had found the wolf for him while Kieran had drunk wine and slept in his luxurious bed. "That wasn't a natural wolf," Alanna said. "It was a Fae-wolf. A Shifter."

"He's a bloody animal. And any Shifter in my realm is fair game."

That was true. No Shifter would venture here on purpose, which meant the Lupine had been captured or lured in somehow. She didn't know enough about Shifters to tell whether the Lupine was male or female, and she wondered if Kieran had stolen its cubs too. She hoped it found its way back to the standing stones and out.

Kieran's hungry gaze went to the sword, the Lupine forgotten. He snapped his fingers at her. Alanna walked to him, handing over the sword and giving him a little curtsy.

"Lovely." Kieran hefted the blade, testing its balance. "This is perfect."

"What is it for?" Alanna asked him.

"Simple, dear sister. To defeat Shifters."

Niall had accused Alanna of knowing what Kieran's spells were for, and she did, but she hadn't understood exactly what Kieran had meant to do with them.

"Defeat them?" she asked. "It's not a good weapon for killing, the Shifter said. Not sturdy enough, even with the spells."

Kieran kept his gaze on the etched blade. "You know that I am named for our grandfather, who was killed by a horde of Lupine Shifters, don't you? Demons in animal skins. I am the legacy of that ancient king called Kieran. With this sword, I shall avenge him."

Alanna felt cold. "How can you? The Shifters who killed him died long ago. Shifters are short-lived, you know; they last only three or four centuries at most. It would be complicated to find their descendants. Shifters have scattered over the human world by now."

Kieran gave her a pitying look. "You are simplistic, my sister. I don't need to find the descendents, I have the Shifters themselves. I have their bones."

He waved his hand and mists lifted from the other side of the clearing. Low mounds, a dozen of them, lay side by side, overgrown with green.

Alanna's eyes widened. "Where did those come from?"

"My loyal men tracked down the graves of the Lupines who slaughtered our grandfather. I had their remains brought here and reburied. I've been collecting them for a long time."

Alanna stared at him in shock. "Why?"

"For this day." Kieran raised the sword again. "Did you not understand the spells I gave you? You are a fine mage, my dear, the only one who wasn't afraid to go to the human world and find the Shifter sword maker. Surely you will have worked it out."

Alanna swallowed. "You wanted to make a soul-stealer."

"Ah, so you have not lost every bit of your intelligence after all. No, I cannot kill the Shifters who murdered our grandfather. But, if I capture their souls and make them do my bidding, they will be miserable for eternity."

Alanna studied the mounds, which looked vulnerable and sad. "But the Shifters have been dead so long. Their souls will be gone—won't they?"

"Not these Shifters. As he killed them, our grandfather cursed their souls to cleave to their dead bones. No going to the happy Summerland to chase rabbits for them."

Alanna hid her revulsion. Even Fae had souls that dissolved when they reached the end of their long lives. The Fae then drifted, content, free of the constrains of the body, which also dissolved. To tie a soul to a cold, dark grave seemed to her the height of barbarity.

"Aren't they miserable already then?" she asked.

"Perhaps, perhaps not. But if *I* have their souls, then they will do my bidding, and they will become aware of their suffering. I will make certain of it."

Alanna shrugged, pretending not to care, even as she shivered deep inside herself. She had to make Kieran believe she sided with him, at least long enough for her purpose. He would kill her afterward, but her task would be complete.

"Well, whatever you intend do with the dogs' souls, the sword maker kept his end of the bargain," she said. "I will take his sons back to the human world."

"I don't bargain with Shifters." Kieran snapped his fingers. "You. Bring the Shifter's get."

Two attendants disappeared and returned holding the squirming cubs, wrapped in nets, in their wildcat forms. Both attendants were cursing as they dropped the bundles to the ground.

"They refuse to shift to human form, Your Highness," one attendant said, breathing hard.

Alanna knelt next to the net-wrapped cubs, keeping herself out of reach of their flailing claws. "Your father sends his love," she whispered. "He says to tell you he's proud of you."

The small cats eyed her in suspicion and kept snarling.

"Let us test the blade on them, shall we?" Kieran said.

Alanna rose to her feet. "You said it wasn't a killing blade."

"No, but it will likely do some damage. They are small, and I imagine their souls will be—cute."

Alanna reached to stop Kieran, and at the same time, a huge Fae-cat tore through the clearing and leapt at them both.

Niall ...

He'd followed her. Alanna watched in panic as the men at arms and attendants attacked him. Niall fought hard, but there were ten Fae to one Shifter, and they quickly overwhelmed him. The men at arms bound him in a net, but Niall went insane, fighting and clawing the ropes, foam and blood flecking his mouth.

Kieran ran at Niall, rage on his face. "I'll test the blade on its maker instead."

Alanna froze in fear, but Niall raged and fought so hard through the net that Kieran couldn't get near him. The men at arms advised their prince to abandon the attempt.

"Tell him to shift back," Kieran shouted at Alanna. "He shifts back or I kill his cubs."

Alanna folded her arms, still striving to pretend she supported him. "Why would he listen to me? I'm Fae. I hope you're happy. He was foul as foul can be the whole time. Shifters disgust me."

Niall roared, the sound booming through the clearing. His children fought and yowled, encouraged by their father's wrath.

"I'll shoot the bastard, instead," Kieran snarled. "Good target practice."

Alanna touched her brother's arm, trying to keep her tone cool. "Why don't you show the Shifter smith what the sword was made for?"

Kieran stopped, and a feral smile creased his face. "Sister, you will make a fine Fae yet. Watch, Shifter. Let me show you how I can reach into the past and hurt you in the present."

The prince's cloak rippled as he strode to the closest mound. He lifted the gleaming silver sword above his head and drove it, point down, straight through the mound.

Light flashed up the length of the sword, and a shower of dirt shot from the grave. A swirl of smoke erupted from the hole in the grave and coalesced into the misty shape of a Fae-wolf.

Kieran laughed. He went to the next mound, and the next, releasing the essences of the Fae-wolves, who formed then floated insubstantially over the places where their bones were buried.

Kieran flourished the sword. "Behold the souls of those who slew my grandfather." He turned to them and opened his arms. "You will surrender to me, and do what I bid. You will kill the Shifter Feline and his cubs."

The figures swirled around him, mist trailing behind them like rags. Alanna held her breath, fingers at her mouth.

This was not what she'd expected to happen. She'd changed the spells as she'd slid them into the sword, repurposing Kieran's magic with her own. She was a good enough mage to do it, to trick him, and she knew it. She'd changed the spells to that a thrust of the sword would release the souls, not enslave them. The wolves should have dispersed, their souls free for all eternity.

Instead the ethereal Lupines lingered, like wolves gathering around prey.

Prey …

"Kieran!" Alanna shouted. "Drop the sword. Run!"

Kieran ignored her. He swept the sword blade through the ghostlike creatures. "Obey, wraiths. Now you are mine."

The wolves circled him, their eyes glowing yellow through the mist. As one, they attacked. Kieran cried out as the pack swept down on him in wild glee, and then he began to scream.

Chapter Seven

Niall shifted to human form, watching in amazement as the ghostly wolves ripped into Kieran. They were mist and smoke—they shouldn't be able to touch him—and yet the wolves tore at him. Kieran's pristine white cloak turned scarlet. His men at arms and attendants, instead of rushing to protect their master, turned in terror and fled.

The sword flew from Kieran's hand, as though it propelled itself, and landed at Niall's feet. Kieran screamed again.

The wolves ripped the prince's body apart, snarls feral as they used teeth and claws to kill. Alanna hugged her arms to her chest, her eyes wide, as her brother slowly died. His screams turned to pleas for mercy, but the wolves did not care.

One wolf finally wrenched out his throat. The Lupine stood back, muzzle covered with blood, triumph in his eyes. At the wolf's feet, Kieran's bloody body folded in on itself and crumpled to dust.

The wolves padded in a circle around the prince's remains, then they lifted their heads and howled. It was a faint whisper of a howl, eerie and hollow, but it held a note of triumph.

The wolves shifted into a dozen men with broad shoulders and flowing hair, with the light blue eyes common to Lupines. They gave Niall and Alanna a collective look of acknowledgment, shifted back into wolves, and vanished. Wisps of smoke spun high into the sky and faded away.

Alanna ran to the fallen sword, caught it up, and rushed to Niall and his cubs. The sword sliced swiftly through the net binding Niall, and then Alanna moved to cut the ropes binding Piers and Marcus.

Both wildcat cubs shifted into boys and ran to Niall, throwing their arms around him. Tears wet Niall's face as he knelt and gathered them in.

He looked over their heads at Alanna, who stood behind them, sword clenched in her hand, her dark eyes wild.

"Alanna," Niall said, trying to stop his voice from shaking. "What happened? What did you do?"

Alanna lifted her chin. "Kieran commanded me to make a soul-stealer, but I spelled the sword to be a soul *releaser*. Instead of binding the souls of those Shifters, driving it through their remains set them free." She drew a shuddering breath, looking white and sick. "At least, that's all I meant to do. I did not realize the Shifters would decide to take their vengeance on Kieran like that. I did not know they *could*."

But as horrifying as Kieran's death had been, Niall couldn't be unhappy that the cruel Fae who'd abducted his children and would have murdered them was gone. "If they hadn't killed him, the prince would have killed all of us."

Alanna nodded. "Me, certainly. I'd hoped that while he attacked me, you and your cubs could get away."

Niall shot to his feet. "That was your plan? For me to run away while you *died*? 'Tis not what Shifters do for mates, lass."

"It's done, Niall. You must leave now. If they find you here, they will hold you responsible. Kieran's cousin, his heir, had no love for Kieran, but he might appease his followers by making an example of you."

Niall hugged his boys close. They were scared, but unhurt, resilient lads. "And what is to say they won't come after me and my cubs into the human world?"

"Because most Fae had no love for Kieran, either," Alanna said. "I doubt any of them will be willing to risk entering the human world to avenge his name."

"But you cannot stay here, either. They'll blame you too."

Alanna gave him a long look. "Perhaps, if you exchanged your steel knives for bronze ones, I could better serve you breakfast?"

Niall's heart thumped fast and hard. He reached for her, pulled her into the circle of his family. "You saved my boys, and me. You stay with me as long as you want. For always is fine with me."

Her scent wrapped him, fresh and graceful and beautiful. Niall wondered that he could have ever disliked it. Wrapping around his heart as well was the warmth of a new bond that had started to forge. The mate bond. He'd teach her how to feel it too.

Alanna held the sword out to him. "This belongs to you."

Niall closed his hand around the hilt. The sword felt right in his palm, as though he'd made it especially for him to hold. And maybe he had. "A soul releaser?"

"I spelled it so that when a Shifter's soul is in peril of being bound to its body or to another's will, this sword will release it in peace. The Lupine souls that had been cursed to linger at their graves have at last gone to the Summerland."

Niall studied the lines and runes that ran up the blade and the hilt. "Why did you do this? Why help Shifters? You're Fae."

"Because many of the Fae are noble people. Some like Kieran, or our grandfather, or the ones who made and enslaved the Shifters in the first place, were cruel—even we consider them cruel. Fae have long lives, and we now live remote from the human world, which makes us view things differently. Kieran's vengeance was that of a child pulling wings from a fly that annoyed him. I could not let him succeed."

The boys were looking at the sword too, with the bright gazes of lads fascinated by a pretty weapon. Niall saw long days ahead explaining to them why they couldn't touch it.

"Why didn't you tell me, lass?" he asked. "When we made the sword together, why didn't you tell me what you were doing?"

"Because when I walked into your forge, you made no secret that you hated Fae. Why should you help me? You are Shifter. And to be honest, I simply didn't think you'd believe me."

"And you'd have been right, love. I wouldn't have." Niall's heart squeezed as he thought of the danger she'd walked into, taking the sword to the Fae realm and knowing her brother would discover what she'd done. "But you should have told me this morning what you intended."

"I *intended* to have your children back to you before you woke. I never thought you'd be daft enough to follow me to Faerie."

"Daft, am I?" Niall tilted her face to his and pressed a brief kiss to her lips. "Who was the one who came here alone, intending to sacrifice herself? But we can argue about who's most foolish later. Let's be going, before your brother's keepers return for us."

They went, through the mists and the standing stones, back to the freezing wind from the wild sea, the light dancing on the waves and the green of the Great Island across the strait. The wind tossed Alanna's hair, which streamed like gold.

They returned to the cottage, where Piers and Marcus ate ravenously and regaled them with their adventures with the enthusiasm of boys no longer afraid. Niall hung the sword point downward on the wall, the blade gleaming softly.

"Keep it well," Alanna said from his kitchen table. "And wield it well."

"There are so many Shifters," Niall said. "I can't be everywhere in the world waiting to see if a Shifter is in danger of losing his soul."

"Then we will make more. We will forge enough swords so that every Shifter clan will have one, and then your work will be done. You aren't the best sword maker alive for nothing."

"I'm so glad you believe in me, lass."

Alanna rose from the table, stepped into his arms, and kissed his lips. Piers and Marcus snickered, children laughing at their elders.

"Of course I believe in you," she said. "But do you believe in me?" Her voice lowered to a whisper. "Have you found the answer to the question you asked last night? Can a Shifter love a Fae?"

Niall cupped her face and looked into her beautiful dark eyes. "If that Fae was you, I think I could. Can you love a Shifter who's covered with soot and smells of iron?"

"I can love you, Niall O'Connell."

"Of course I won't be home much, if you expect me to forge a sword for every Shifter clan in existence."

Alanna gave him a smile that showed him her strength as well as her compassion. "We'll do it together. Every piece, every hammer stroke, we'll forge them together."

"Sounds like bliss, that does. Or a lot of bloody work."

"But worth it?"

"Aye, love." Niall sank into her warmth, took her mouth in a long kiss, ignoring his sons' gleeful laughter. Laughter meant love, and he'd take it. "'Twill be well worth it."

END

About the Author

New York Times bestselling and award-winning author Jennifer Ashley has written more than 45 published novels and novellas in romance, urban fantasy, and mystery under the names Jennifer Ashley, Allyson James, and Ashley Gardner. Her books have been nominated for and won Romance Writers of America's RITA (given for the best romance novels and novellas of the year), several *RT BookReviews* Reviewers Choice awards (including Best Urban Fantasy, Best Historical Mystery, and Career Achievement in Historical Romance). Jennifer's books have been translated into a dozen different languages and have earned starred reviews in *Booklist.*

More about the Shifters Unbound series can be found at www.jennifersromances.com. Or email Jennifer at jenniferashley@cox.net

Books in the Shifters Unbound series
Pride Mates
Primal Bonds
Bodyguard
Wild Cat
Mate Claimed
And more to come!

Books in the Mackenzies series
The Madness of Lord Ian Mackenzie
Lady Isabella's Scandalous Marriage
The Many Sins of Lord Cameron
The Duke's Perfect Wife
The Seduction of Elliot McBride
And more to come!